### "My nec

Michael opened his eyes with a start. He'd heard Jillian speak, but how could she speak when her mouth was engaged with his? Worse, her discomfort had yanked him from his dreamy daze. He was about to suggest a change of position…

"Maybe if I bend my head his way… There, that's better."

The hairs rose along Michael's skin as he stared down at her. Some barely functioning part of his brain registered that while he'd heard her words, her mouth hadn't actually moved—it was still occupied with his.

He even managed to keep his eyes open and his gaze on her face when she said, "I know what'll make him get this show on the road."

With a deft stroke of Jillian's fingers, the vestiges of Michael's reason collided with raw sensation, and he finally pulled together what was happening.

Michael wasn't hearing what Jillian was saying, because she wasn't talking.…

As impossible as it might seem, he was actually hearing what she was *thinking!*

# Blaze™

Dear Reader,

I married my husband because he was my hero come to life—romantic, handsome and oh, so charming. We've crammed a lot of life into the eighteen years since the wedding, and while reality might have worn off some of the polish, my hero is still alive and well. When I least expect it, he scoops me into his arms, grins sexily and says, "You are just too cute."

And manages to make me feel cute.

That's why I was so enamored with the idea of writing about renewing the passion in marriage. While time might dull a bit of the shine, that same time can foster a trust and familiarity that are perfect to explore fantasies we might otherwise consider *forbidden*....

Drop me a line at Harlequin Enterprises Limited, 225 Duncan Mill Road, Don Mills, Ontario M3B 3K9, Canada or visit my Web site at www.jeanielondon.com.

Very truly yours,

*Jeanie London*

# IF YOU COULD
# READ MY MIND...
## *Jeanie London*

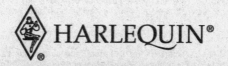

HARLEQUIN®

TORONTO • NEW YORK • LONDON
AMSTERDAM • PARIS • SYDNEY • HAMBURG
STOCKHOLM • ATHENS • TOKYO • MILAN • MADRID
PRAGUE • WARSAW • BUDAPEST • AUCKLAND

ISBN-13: 978-0-373-79275-7
ISBN-10:    0-373-79275-1

IF YOU COULD READ MY MIND...

This edition published by arrangement with Harlequin Books S.A.

® and TM are trademarks of the publisher. Trademarks indicated with ® are registered in the United States Patent and Trademark Office, the Canadian Trade Marks Office and in other countries.

www.eHarlequin.com

**Printed in U.S.A.**

## ABOUT THE AUTHOR

Jeanie London writes romances because she believes in happily-ever-afters. Not the "love conquers all" kind, but the "we love each other, so we can conquer anything" kind. She writes red-hot romance and romantic suspense for Harlequin and paranormal romance for Tor. She's been blessed with numerous writing awards and a husband who has her wondering if he can read her mind. What else could explain the stellar job he's done fulfilling her most forbidden fantasies?

## Books by Jeanie London

### HARLEQUIN BLAZE

### HARLEQUIN SIGNATURE SELECT SPOTLIGHT

*Falling Inn Bed…
†Red Letter Nights

To my very own hero—*always*.
Happy anniversary, honey!

# *Prologue*

*When the trouble first started*

EXACTLY *why* had she fallen in love with this man again? Right now, Jillian Landry honestly couldn't remember, which was saying something since *this man* was her husband of seven years. Before marriage she'd dated him for five years and, before that, tagged after him for the better part of her life. Ever since the day her older brother had returned from kindergarten to proclaim Michael Landry as his new best friend.

But at the moment…after being restrained in said husband's dental chair, Jillian couldn't remember what she'd ever seen in a man who'd obviously lost his mind between the time he'd locked up the clinic after the staff's departure and his return trip.

"Michael, what are you doing?"

Flipping off the overhead fluorescent lights, he shot her a smile that dazzled in the suddenly dim room. "I'm creating a fantasy for you. You said you wanted a fantasy, remember?"

Oh, she remembered all right. The whole idea of fantasies had come up during a conversation at a recent Main Street Rehabilitation fund-raiser. She and Michael had been chatting with the Prestons during cocktail hour, when

Amelia Preston—a society matron with enough money to discuss whatever was on her mind—began an interrogation about how to keep the romance alive in a marriage.

Jillian hadn't been sure whether Amelia had been grilling guests for tidbits to spice up her own decades-old marriage or the dull pre-dinner party. Whatever the motivation, she'd succeeded in getting Jillian to consider the question in the car on the way home.

No denying that after seven years of marriage, there'd been some trade-off of excitement for predictability. Not necessarily a bad thing, she'd been quick to point out. Orgasms were better than ever because practice made perfect. After so much practice, Michael was a locksmith with all the right keys.

But she'd admitted to seeing the appeal of a little fantasy now and then to keep the romance alive.

Apparently *now* was *then*.

The best Michael could come up with was handcuffs?

"Are you open for something different tonight, Jilly?" Michael shrugged off his white lab coat to reveal the shirt and pants she'd just picked up from the cleaners yesterday.

"Dare I ask how different?"

He strode purposefully toward her, his smile promising a satisfying answer to her question. "How about you just stick around to find out?"

*Stick around?*

Testing the steel restraining her to his dental chair, the very one his last patient had vacated not a half hour earlier, Jillian had to wonder where he thought she could go.

She wouldn't ask where he'd gotten the handcuffs. Michael cared for the smiles of over half the police force in their hometown of Natchez, Mississippi. And those spit-polished good old boys—most of whom were lifelong friends—would be smiling if they knew why Michael wanted restraints. Just the thought was enough to make her wince.

Or maybe the crick in her neck was to blame.

Or her numb arm and tingling fingers.

"How about you just relax and trust me to show you a good time?" Michael loomed over her, blue eyes glinting with sexy innuendo, and slipped his hands beneath her uniform smock.

His warm fingers caressed her skin with tantalizing slowness as he eased the hem up, up, up, until he bared her bra to his gaze.

With that smile still playing around his lips, he descended, his mouth making contact with her skin to trail moist kisses in the wake of his hands.

"That feels nice."

"You just wait." His words broke against her skin in breathy bursts then, in one skilled move, he popped open the fastener on her bra.

Her breasts tumbled free, nipples puckering at contact with the climate-controlled air. Michael was there instantly, dragging his warm tongue over one peak in an arousing stroke, easing his fingers around the other and weighing her in his warm palm.

Willing herself to relax, Jillian forced her focus onto her husband's sexy ministrations and not the dull throb of her shoulder. She supposed there'd been no other place to attach the handcuffs besides the mechanism under the chair arm. She might have suggested something more user-friendly had Michael not taken her by surprise by cuffing her here in the first place.

Now, she didn't want to say anything he might perceive as a lack of enthusiasm. He wanted to create a fantasy tonight, and as she'd been the one to pursue Amelia Preston's conversation...

But Jillian couldn't help wondering if Michael had taken action on that conversation because he'd noticed the trade-off between excitement and predictability, too.

Surely all the passion couldn't have gone after only seven years of marriage?

Of course not.

Through sheer determination, Jillian forced all her focus onto the feel of Michael's mouth on her, the caress of his warm hands, the promise of an orgasm that was bound to leave her gasping.

Arching her back slightly, she lifted her breasts in an eager posture and bullied her libido into a response.

And there it was...a life sign.

Awareness flickered deep inside, and she closed her eyes to shut out everything but the feel of Michael's mouth, the swirl of his tongue, the slow pull of his lips.

He let his hands join the game, pinching her nipples as if recognizing he'd have to break out the heavy artillery to coax her body to life after such an exhausting day.

A few firm squeezes did the trick. Her insides melted, and desire pooled warmly between her thighs.

"Mmm." She exhaled the sigh on a breath.

"Like that, do you?" Michael sounded very pleased with her response.

"You know I do."

He squeezed again, this time earning a shiver. "I can think of a few other things you like, too."

"Be still my heart."

He chuckled. "Uh-uh, Jilly. There's going to be nothing still about you by the time I'm through."

To prove his point, he caught the elastic waistband of her pants and tugged them over her hips and down her legs. Then he reared back and raked a hungry gaze over her.

"As gorgeous as ever." He dragged his fingertips lightly over her stomach, a teasing touch that made her tremble. Then he toyed with the edge of her cotton panties, easing his fingers inside just enough to make her sound breathless when she said, "I'm very glad you think so."

"Oh, I do, my beautiful bride. I do." To prove his point, he gazed down pointedly at his crotch, drawing her attention to the promising bulge there.

"If I had free hands, I'd undress you, too."

"Allow me."

She thought he might free her, but he began a careful striptease instead. So, lying in his dental chair, nearly naked and definitely aroused, she watched him peel away clothes that showed the effects of the long day to reveal all the tantalizing secrets below.

He was just thirty-two, two years older than she was, and she could still see the boy she'd fallen in love with inside this more mature version. He'd been the high-school football star. The handsome homecoming king. The proud fraternity president. A devastatingly romantic groom.

Jillian still felt a tingle when she thought about all those yummy memories, still admired his strong features, the glossy black hair that contrasted so sharply with his blue eyes.

*Michael.*

She'd been involved with him for most of her life. She supposed it was only natural that their relationship ebbed and flowed. They'd weather this lull just as they'd weathered tough years during college and dental school and a financially difficult start to his practice.

Of course they would.

# 1

*Several weeks later*

THE WHINING of the high-speed drill hadn't faded to silence before Michael Landry heard his wife say, "I'm leaving now."

Glancing up from his patient, who reclined in the dental chair with his open mouth exposing a problem molar, Michael found Jillian standing in the doorway. He couldn't help but smile at the sight of her, looking all brisk and businesslike in her colorful smock and white pants.

She wore the same uniform as his staff, although she'd applied her business degree toward managing his office ever since he'd set up his practice after dental school. Several years might have passed since they'd bought this old building in downtown Natchez, but Jillian looked the same as the sparkling-eyed young girl he'd fallen in love with so long ago.

She was still the most beautiful woman he'd ever seen.

Strawberry-blond hair waved around her face, and she had warm brown eyes that could melt with pleasure or twinkle with laughter. She could still catch him off guard with her smile.

"You remember we have an interview with the caretakers from New Orleans at the camp tonight," she said.

"What time is it again?" He wasn't about to admit he hadn't remembered.

"Seven. If you lock up right after your last patient and leave with the staff, you should have plenty of time to get through traffic."

"To Camp Cavelier?" Louis Bernard lifted his head from the headrest, almost nailing the equipment tray before Michael made a quick save. "You'll make the camp by seven if you're driving on the shoulder up State Road Twenty."

"Not if he leaves with the staff," Jillian said firmly. "Are you sure you don't want me to wait for you?"

"You said you needed to look over their paperwork. Go ahead. I'll be there."

He could hear Charlotte snicker from behind her paper mask and shot his nurse a look he hoped would deter her from comment. He was already in enough hot water with Jillian about their latest investment venture.

But Charlotte O'Brien wasn't in the habit of being deterred by him. This sixty-ish, pixie-ish dynamo had been a nurse since long before Michael had even thought about going into dentistry. She had a lot of know-how, and despite their years together, he still hadn't decided why she worked for him. Some days he thought she was impressed with his skill and chair-side manner. Other days, he suspected she felt it was her duty to tell him what to do to keep his patients safe.

She didn't even bother trying to hide her amusement now. "What your wife wants here is confirmation. Go on and tell her you'll let us drag you out the door when we leave before she gets a gray hair."

"Now that's where you're wrong." He slid his stool back

and stood. "Jillian's just doing what she always does—keeping my schedule straight so I can devote myself to my patients. Don't know what I'd do without this woman."

He caught her around the waist and waltzed her through the cramped space in the exam room. With a gasp, she melted into his arms the way she always did, as if her luscious body had been designed exclusively to fit close.

"Michael!"

"Yes, my beautiful bride?"

"You're crazy."

"Only about you, love of my life."

"Oh, Michael."

He whirled her to the sound of Charlotte's chuckles and Louis's deep-throated guffaws. Unable to resist, he dipped her over his arm for good measure, one of those dramatic, romantic gestures that never failed to make Jillian sigh those breathless sighs that caught him hard in the gut.

She melted over his arm in a liquid move and exhaled a gasping laugh. That had been the first thing to attract him to Jillian—her laughter. Unrestrained, glorious laughter. He couldn't resist kissing the sound from her lips.

So, flipping up his paper mask, he did.

Her mouth yielded beneath his, her kiss so natural and welcoming that he felt that twist low in his gut. He resisted the urge to deepen their kiss and taste the sweet greeting he knew would be his.

That was the way it had always been between them—*right*. Ever since he'd stolen his first kiss on the high-school football field after a particularly tight win, he'd responded to Jillian in a way he had no other.

He still did. She was such a tidy armful with her hands

wound around his neck to hang on, her warm breaths clashing with his in easy rhythm. She made him think about sex.

They only parted after attracting an audience. His two hygienists stood in the hall beyond the open doorway, their applause muffled by their sanitary gloves.

"Show's over, folks." He waved everyone back to work.

With laughing comments, his staff disbanded, and Jillian rolled her eyes, pecked him on the cheek and said, "Now back to work before you get totally off schedule."

"Or my anesthetic wears off." Louis shot a worried glance at the drill.

Michael got back to his own work before Louis's anesthetic did indeed wear off. He pointedly ignored the amusement glinting in Charlotte's eyes above the mask.

He wasn't entirely sure how he'd earned this open conspiracy, but his wife and office staff had taken it upon themselves to point him through his days as if he couldn't find his own way. If it made them all feel useful to play mother hens, then Michael tried not to complain.

He could think of a lot worse things than a bunch of women caring about him.

Not to mention that Charlotte made the best damn fried chicken he'd ever tasted. He wouldn't do anything to risk ticking her off and denying himself those little plastic baggies filled with crispy drumsticks.

Even their newest hygienist, Brandi, young as she was, had followed suit, to become his newest mother hen. And Michael chose to let these ladies do what made them happy. Most of the time keeping his ladies happy made him happy, too, but there were days when their hovering got annoying.

Like at the end of the long work day when he and the staff were leaving the office.

Michael patted his back pocket. "Damn, I forgot my wallet. Knowing my luck, I'll get pulled over and not have my license."

"Go on and get it." Charlotte reached out to grab the door from him. "I'll wait."

Being mother-henned was one thing. Being made to feel incompetent was another entirely. "Thanks, but if you don't get to Libby's dance recital before the theater fills up, you'll never get a decent seat."

There was no argument there, but he could tell Charlotte didn't want to leave until she saw him get inside his car.

"Jillian said to make sure you leave with us, Michael," Dianne informed him.

"I only have to grab my wallet," he informed his senior hygienist.

"You'll only be a minute?" Charlotte frowned at him.

He frowned right back, and she obviously recognized that he was only half joking.

"See you tomorrow, ladies. I'm quite capable of grabbing my wallet and making it to my car without an escort."

That the ladies didn't look convinced annoyed him further.

"Enjoy the recital, Charlotte," he prompted. "You two have a good night, as well."

"G'night, Michael."

Charlotte forced a smile and headed to her car.

Shaking his head, he wound his way through the space, flipping on lights as he went, finally reaching his private office at the rear of the building.

What made these women think he needed a babysitter?

Circling his desk, he retrieved his wallet from the drawer. He really didn't have an answer to the question, but knew he'd simply have to weather the storm, which meant getting on the road. Glancing up at the wall clock, he found himself ten minutes ahead of schedule.

What had Charlotte been worried about?

Slipping his wallet inside his back pocket, Michael reached for his handheld recorder. He typically dictated his patients' reports before leaving the office at the end of the day, while the information was still fresh in his head.

His medical transcriptionist came in for a few hours each morning. He could give her a few to start with in the morning, which would buy him time to dictate the rest. He glanced at the files stacked neatly on the edge of his desk. In ten minutes he could dictate at least two. With any luck, three....

JILLIAN WATCHED the old-model Lincoln Town Car wind down the long dirt drive toward the camp, kicking up clouds of dust into the twilight. The sun set in pastel strands over the Mississippi, and from her perch on the bluff, she let the quiet river soothe away her annoyance that Michael hadn't shown up before the interview as she'd asked him to.

She'd decided to reserve judgment about why he wasn't here. Jillian knew if an emergency had come up at the last minute he wouldn't have hesitated to place a patient in his chair. Michael had the biggest heart of anyone she'd ever known, which was one of the things she loved best about him. He cared about what he did, so much so that she'd been forced to reevaluate their office system four times to figure out how to squeeze so many patients into one man's schedule.

Jillian frowned. If an emergency had come up, Charlotte would have called.

She hoped he hadn't had any trouble on the road or, God forbid, an accident. Just the thought was enough to erase the calming effects of the sunset and trap the breath in her chest.

But, Jillian reasoned, if Michael had had an accident, he'd have called. Or *someone* would have. They knew so many state troopers and emergency personnel around town that someone could have tracked her down if something horrible had happened.

But just in case, Jillian glanced inside her purse to make sure her cell phone was on. Yes, the phone was on and, yes, the battery was sufficiently charged. She resisted the urge to call him. The office phones rolled over to the answering service when the staff left. Even if his personal cell phone was on, which she knew it wouldn't be, Jillian would only frustrate herself. Michael had said he would be here. She'd simply trust he had a good reason for not calling to say he was running late.

That was the last chance she got to dwell on Michael, anyway, because the old blue Lincoln pulled into the circle drive, following signs leading it straight to the office where she stood on the porch beneath a slightly sagging overhang.

This log cabin had been built by Camp Cavelier's original owners and had seen every season since the camp had opened on this Mississippi bluff. She and Michael were the camp's first owners who were not actually members of the founding family. It was a position that came with historic obligation and a lot of tradition, responsibilities Jillian intended to live up to.

But as she was learning firsthand since assuming the

role, she needed help. *Full-time* help. And an up-close glimpse of the Lincoln coming to a stop in front of the stairs wasn't inspiring much confidence. She smiled as the doors swung wide and the members of the Baptiste family from a bayou town south of New Orleans emerged.

These people were clearly related. Three shared glossy black hair; all shared dark eyes, elegantly refined features and deep gold skin. The distance of generations didn't dim the beauty of these people. She had to force her gaze from the two young men and their sister to greet the elderly woman, who made Jillian hope to look so good at seventy-something.

Of course, this beautiful older woman also looked as if she'd just stepped off a Mardi Gras float, dressed as she was in a roomy skirt in Day-Glo orange and a shawl of a complementary yellow only slightly less radiant than the sun. To complete the ensemble, she'd woven matching ribbons through her hair, pulling the wildly curling gray locks back from her face.

"Mrs. Baptiste-Mercier, it's a pleasure. I'm Jillian Landry. We spoke on the phone." Smiling her most welcoming smile, she stepped off the last riser and extended her hand.

"Call me Widow Serafine." The woman's smooth round face split into deep creases as she smiled and she clasped Jillian's with a strength that matched her size. "Every one else does. And you're as pretty as I knew you'd be. I said to myself, 'Serafine, any lady with that warm honey voice is surely Southern and one real beauty.'"

Her smoky gaze took Jillian's measure in a frank glance, and there was something penetrating, almost fierce about the look. But her smile widened, leaving Jillian feeling sure about the compliment.

"Thank you." She turned her attention to the three younger Baptistes, who clustered around Widow Serafine in pack-like fashion. "These are your…grandchildren?"

She hadn't been entirely clear on the relationship from their one and only telephone conversation.

Widow Serafine shook her head. "Of a sort. My sister Virginie's brood. Baptistes through and through, even if they haven't accepted it yet." She motioned to one, a roguishly attractive young man with a guarded expression. "Raphael's the oldest. He's twenty. Has a way with horses and cars. And his kin. He keeps them in line. Don't know what I'd do without him, truth be told. This here's Philip, the middle— Come on, boy, pay your respects to Mrs. Jillian."

Mrs. Jillian?

*Okay.*

Philip sidled forward with the lanky grace of a boy who hadn't quite grown into his body yet. He eyed her with an inscrutable expression, and she smiled in reply.

"Marie-Louise is the baby. She's just graduated from high school, but she won't turn eighteen until the end of the month. Hope that won't be a problem." She frowned. "I can sign any documents so she can work legal until then if need be. Wouldn't want to cause you any trouble."

Jillian wasn't worried about trouble, or documents, which seemed to be jumping the gun when they hadn't yet interviewed.

Lucky for her, she didn't have to figure out how to diplomatically address this oversight because Widow Serafine herded her "sort-of" granddaughter to the front of the pack so Jillian got a good look.

"Marie-Louise will help me keep up the place," Widow

Serafine explained. "And cook. She's a right Rachael Ray—talented, sensible and pretty as sin. Loves to work in the kitchen while she's daydreaming about falling in love." Widow Serafine winked. "Giving her brothers a run for their money keeping the young bucks away, I tell you."

To confirm her statement, Raphael scowled. Philip nodded.

Marie-Louise just smiled, an easy smile that Jillian liked straight away. She was young, but such a beauty with that glossy black hair curling around her oval face and those almond-shaped eyes. Her sundress was simple and stylish, not suggestive like so many of the juniors' fashions nowadays. Even so, it couldn't hide a body that the young bucks would no doubt go ga-ga for.

"I'm pleased to meet you all," Jillian said. "Shall we tour the place before it gets dark? I can tell you about the camp and what's involved with the caretaking jobs."

Before she moved off the bottom step or even opened her mouth to launch into a rehearsed spiel about how Camp Cavelier resided on fifty peaceful acres nestled between the Mississippi River and Lake Lily, Jillian found herself staring at the back of Widow Serafine's head as she motioned to the car.

"Mrs. Jillian's going to take us around. Let's get those groceries settled in the fridge so we don't attract every raccoon hungry enough to smell supper."

Groceries?

Jillian watched in growing amazement as Raphael popped open the trunk and his younger siblings crowded around to unload what turned out to be exactly what Widow Serafine claimed. Groceries, and a week's worth by the looks of it.

Had this woman misunderstood the telephone conversation? Could she possibly have confused being *interviewed* with being *hired* for the caretaking positions?

Jillian had been quite clear on the point, she was sure, but before she had a chance to question the elder Baptiste, she found herself holding a paper sack filled with what appeared to be a healthy variety of fruits and vegetables.

"Would you mind?" Widow Serafine asked. "Didn't think that cottage you mentioned on the phone would have a stocked pantry, so we stopped by the market on the way through town. Now where will we be setting up house?"

This was a perfect time to address the misunderstanding. Jillian would simply explain that she'd envisioned moving this process along more traditional lines starting with an interview then following up on references before committing to employment.

That was certainly how she'd conducted business in the past when hiring staff for Michael's practice or appointing people to various board positions on the Main Street Rehabilitation project. The process was tried and true and had always served her well. Obviously the Baptistes did things differently in the bayou.

And exactly where was Michael when she could have used his help? He'd have turned on that high-beam smile and charmed this old granny, buying Jillian some time to figure out how best to handle this unexpected situation.

As it was, she stood there wide-eyed and speechless—a rarity for someone not prone to wide eyes or speechlessness.

Widow Serafine proved much more astute because she clearly recognized the trouble and countered by launching into the tale of what had led her family to Camp Cavelier.

Hurricane Katrina.

When the storm had taken a turn at the last possible second to spare New Orleans a direct hit, landfall had happened directly over Bayou Doré—the Baptistes' world for the better part of two centuries since they'd worked for the privateer Captain Lefever.

Widow Serafine stood there with her sister's grandkids all clutching grocery sacks, and explained how the family had been rebuilding ever since the hurricane. But these three children had been so unsettled that they hadn't seemed to be helping to make a difficult situation any better.

According to her, Raphael, Philip and Marie-Louise had never entirely settled in with the family in the five years since their granny had passed. They seemed to have taken on Virginie's onus as black sheep and held it close no matter how friendly and inviting their extended family had been.

Widow Serafine explained that when she had seen Jillian's ad for camp caretakers, she knew this was exactly what these three kids needed—a place to call their own. Virginie had raised her grandkids on a huge working ranch near Shreveport where she'd been the housekeeper.

With the stables and outdoor work, Camp Cavelier would be a familiar-type place where these black-sheep Baptistes could finally settle in. A place that would give them a purpose. And Widow Serafine had left her home to come with them because that was her duty to her baby sister.

The fact that Jillian hadn't yet offered them the jobs didn't appear to be of concern.

Before she could address that singularly important issue, Widow Serafine paused in her tale to draw a breath, fixed her gaze absently above Jillian's head and said, "Well, that roof won't hold up through the first summer rain. Philip worked with my son-in-law's roofing company during the summer between ninth and tenth grades. He'll get right on that. You hear, Philip?"

"I hear, Widow."

While balancing her armful of groceries, Widow Serafine reached out a hand and beaned Philip on the back of the head, hard enough to make him wince. "Show some respect, boy."

Philip peered over his bags, looking embarrassed but contrite. "I'll get to fixing that roof straight away, ma'am."

Jillian inclined her head, not trusting herself to open her mouth, not when she felt as if she'd been run over by a train.

"Looks like more than that roof will need to be fixed around here," Raphael added. "We saw the sign out at the road. The whole thing's rotting out."

Jillian didn't get a chance to reply before Widow Serafine informed her proudly, "When Raphael isn't working on cars, he works with my son who does carpentry and millwork."

It certainly sounded as if the young man was a hard worker, and Jillian forced herself to look casual, knew she needed to do more than stare and let Widow Serafine run roughshod over her. Even if a sinking feeling in the pit of her stomach warned she wouldn't easily sidestep this old granny's strong will.

"Your application says you have experience with horses, too, Raphael," she said cordially.

"I've been a stable assistant since I've been six years old, ma'am. Well, until we moved in with the widow."

"He has a way with horses. This one does." Widow

Serafine nodded in approval. "Shame we didn't have any in Bayou Doré. But Raphael branched out and learned new skills."

"That's always a good idea," was all Jillian thought to say.

"Looks like you need a jack-of-all-trades around here."

There was no denying Widow Serafine's statement, so Jillian just smiled, buying herself more time to figure out how best to redirect this conversation.

No such luck.

"You have a whole stable full here at the camp, don't you, ma'am?" Raphael asked. "Read on the Internet that you teach the campers how to ride all summer long."

"You researched the camp on the Web?"

"Needed to know the place before we sent in our applications," Raphael said.

Jillian couldn't miss the gravity in those simple words. This young man took his responsibilities very seriously. In her preliminary research of this family, she'd spoken to the ranch owner where these kids had grown up. The man had assured her the Baptistes had been a family of dedicated workers, which was why she'd scheduled this initial interview.

Or what was supposed to have been an interview.

"Your Web site had most of the information," Raphael continued. "Found out Camp Cavelier is the oldest resident camp on the Mississippi. It was named after the man who led the expedition that made the first documented contact between the Natchez Indians and Europeans."

"That's right," she said. "Rene Robert Cavelier."

"Told you the boy was enterprising," Widow Serafine proclaimed proudly.

The fact that this young man had been thorough enough to research the camp certainly seemed to bear up that claim. Jillian wasn't sure if she felt better about the situation or not, but when they all fell silent, she knew they were waiting for her to make the next move.

What could she say? "Take your groceries and go back to the hurricane-ravaged bayou where you came from?"

So she stood there, clutching her own bag in the growing darkness, staring at her interviewees and recognizing the fierce pride in their manner.

That sinking feeling in her stomach eased up a bit.

This was apparently one of those times when things weren't going to work out exactly as planned. She would simply have to have faith that there was a reason, and that reason would turn out to be a good one.

"Well then, if you'll follow me," Jillian finally said, managing to sound normal. "The cottage is just past the cabins."

"Lead the way." Widow Serafine's eyes twinkled.

Jillian couldn't help but wonder what she'd just gotten herself into. She also wondered what Michael would think about this unusual situation.

Or if he would think about it at all.

She knew the answer to that question—no. If she didn't tell him about it, he'd never know. And since he hadn't been here, he'd just have to live with her decision, wouldn't he?

# 2

NIGHT HAD FALLEN by the time Michael finally steered his SUV past Camp Cavelier's weatherworn sign. His headlights sliced through the darkness to illuminate the winding dirt road and throw the surrounding forest into gloom.

During the drive, he'd imagined several scenarios at arriving nearly two hours late for Jillian's interview—all of them involving a very unhappy Jillian. But dealing with her annoyance wasn't his primary concern at the moment. Not when he pulled up to find the office dark.

He'd have to find her to know how annoyed she was.

Circling into the lot in front of the building, Michael pulled his SUV beside a Lincoln Town Car that had seen better days. Most likely the potential caretakers. He put his car into Park and got out.

He didn't think Jillian would tour people through the camp in the dark. Even flashlights wouldn't afford enough light to see much, as he well knew from combing these woods as a kid.

Camp Cavelier was an institution. So many campers flew in from all over the country that the camp ran a shuttle service to the airport. Most local kids, too, spent summers as resident campers. He and Jillian had been no exception, which was precisely why he was now an owner of the property.

A grudging owner, he amended.

Jillian and her causes—they'd be the death of him yet.

Shaking his head, Michael headed up the steps, hoping she'd left a note and some clue as to where he could find her. He was in enough hot water without wasting more time hunting her down. Then something caught his eye…

Her purse.

She'd left it sitting on the bench, and he flipped it open to find her car keys and cell phone inside, which explained why she hadn't been answering her phone. He viewed the display. Sure enough, there was a log of her four missed messages.

All from him.

Damn it, but he should never have sat back at his desk tonight. He should have grabbed his wallet and headed out, as he'd told Charlotte he'd do. Or he should have accepted Jillian's offer to wait for him to make the drive together.

Or maybe they should never have taken on this camp at all. They were just too busy to do right by the place.

The presence of the unfamiliar car drove home a sharp reminder that the interviewees were strangers. Michael's only consolation was that she wasn't entirely alone on the property. Camp Cavelier was more than a seasonal camp—these hallowed acres also played home to a small working farm. Year round, schools scheduled field trips, various organizations booked group tours and families hosted children's birthday parties.

Ike Fleming had been running the farm since Michael

and Jillian had taken their own school field trips. He was even older today than he'd seemed back then, which was saying something since he'd always looked seriously old and seriously big—a mountain of a man. But he was a warm body, at least, and a warm body that packed a loaded shotgun when patrolling the area at night.

Of course, Ike's eyesight had to be failing by now....

An inspection of the office didn't yield up any note from Jillian. Job applications scattered over a desk, assuring him that she'd stuck to her original plan. Helping himself to a flashlight, he locked her purse in his car then took off in the direction of Ike's cottage on the south side of Lake Lily.

The dark night didn't bring back memories of summers spent boating, horseback-riding or working the farm, although he had many. As a young camper, he'd not only communed with nature and wildlife in a place where technology wasn't allowed, but had formed friendships that had weathered the passage of time.

Including a love affair with his wife.

But tonight Michael wasn't remembering when he and Jillian had ducked out of a trail ride to make out in the hayloft, or the time they'd stolen out of the cabins late at night to skinny-dip in the lake.

No, tonight these well-worn trails only yielded grisly images of what could happen to a woman alone in the dark. By the time Michael saw the dull glow of Ike's porch light, his heart was pounding unnaturally hard.

"Ike," he called, knocking on the door. "It's Michael. You in there?"

No response.

Michael waited on the doorstep, growing more agitated with each passing second.

"Ike!" He pounded harder this time. Looked like Ike's hearing was going, too.

Nothing.

Impatiently, Michael tried the handle to find the door unlocked. He pushed inside, calling out loudly as he did, but it didn't take long to realize that no one was home.

Yet Ike had obviously left in a hurry because a full coffee cup—now stone-cold—sat on the table beside an open newspaper.

The shotgun rack above the sofa was empty.

Michael was getting a bad feeling. He couldn't be sure whether guilt or the darkness fueled his imagination, but his head raced with every horror story he'd ever seen in the news.

Had Jillian gotten into trouble? Had Ike taken the shotgun out to rescue her?

Had the old guy succeeded?

Racking his brain to remember what Jillian had told him about her interviewees, Michael found himself cursing that he hadn't paid closer attention. But Camp Cavelier was Jillian's pet project and he'd apparently only listened with one ear.

Guilt, definitely.

Heading back outside, he pulled the door shut behind him. Sounds from the stabled horses and forest wildlife filtered through the darkness, and he made his way to the trail. He'd circle around to the cabins. It was the only thing to do. There were cars, which meant Jillian was somewhere.

He'd damn sure find her.

Something crashed in the underbrush, startling the night

quiet and drawing Michael to a sharp stop. With his heart-beat spiking hard, he waited for something—Ike, wildlife or a murderer?—to appear on the path ahead.

As the seconds ticked past, stillness settled over the night again.

He came upon the boys' cabins first, and the rustic structures that had once seemed so offhandedly inviting now loomed eerily empty in the moonlight. There were no windows in these cabins, only screens to keep out the snakes and spiders. No air-conditioning, either, which made the bunks inside a stifling ride during the sultry summer.

He mentally rattled off the cabin's names by rote: Company Thirteen. Pirates. Lightning Bolt. Dreadnought. Wave Runners. Hackers.

"Jillian," he called out then waited to hear a reply, or any sound to indicate she was in trouble and needed help.

Nothing.

Making his way toward the girls' cabins, he stumbled over what he belatedly realized was the ring of stones surrounding the bonfire pit. He almost landed face first inside a crater filled with winter-rotted leaves and ash.

He caught his balance at the last possible second, but dropped the flashlight.

"Oh, man." He sank his fingers into the decomposing debris to retrieve the flashlight, which had managed to bury itself deeply enough to cut off the light.

An owl hooted sharply.

"I don't need this grief," he informed the wildlife. "I knew this camp was going to be trouble the instant Jillian came home with the idea."

Not only had the investment run their credit dry, but the workload was creating conflict in their otherwise perfect lives.

Scowling into the darkness, Michael heard another sound, so faint at first that he might have imagined it.

Laughter?

He didn't think it was a cry for help.

Rooted to the spot, he tried to make out the sound, but the night had fallen silent. Then he heard it again.

Laughter, definitely.

Following the direction of the sound, he found himself following the trail around the cabins toward the river.

What would Jillian be doing out on the bluff…? Then Michael saw light glowing through the darkness.

The caretaker's cottage.

With a tentative sense of relief, he headed down the winding dirt path until he found soft light glowing from open windows and heard the sounds of more laughter.

And a fiddle?

Yes, a fiddle. He bolted up the porch steps and knocked loudly on the door.

He had to knock again to be heard, but finally a rather round woman with curly gray hair pulled open the door and broke into a big smile.

"Well hello, handsome. I don't suppose you're looking for me, since I just got here."

The young man playing the fiddle screeched to a halt, but before Michael could reply, he heard Jillian's silvery laughter.

There she was, standing by the kitchen sink with an apron around her waist. While he'd been getting an ulcer on his midnight tour of the camp, she was having a party.

The trade-off seemed wrong in the extreme.

"Heya, Michael." Ike sat at the picnic-style dining table with the shotgun propped beside him. "You tracked us down."

"Good evening, Ike." Michael flipped off the flashlight. "I dropped by your place, too, looking for my beautiful bride."

Jillian wiped her hands on the dish towel and joined him. "Widow Serafine, this is my husband, Michael."

"The dentist," said the woman with the unusual name, eyeing him with an approving smile.

He nodded. "I take it we have new caretakers."

"In fact, we do."

Given Jillian's thorough screening process, he hadn't expected this problem to be solved anytime soon. But when she introduced the younger generation of the Baptiste family, he thought the group seemed a nice enough bunch.

After exchanging greetings, Widow Serafine motioned him inside the kitchen. "Are you hungry, Dr. Michael? Marie-Louise whipped us up a welcome feast. You need to sit yourself down and get some before it's all gone. Got growing boys around here." She eyed Ike, who rubbed his stomach appreciatively.

Michael hadn't ever seen Ike smile that widely, and his own stomach growled, recalling how long it had been since lunch. Casting Jillian a sidelong glance, he gauged her mood while deciding whether to deal with the issue between them now or wait until later when they were alone.

One way or the other, he'd better address his tardiness.

Since her honey-gold eyes didn't give him a clue to what was happening behind them, he decided on the path of the least resistance.

Pressing a kiss to her cheek, he said, "Sorry, Jilly. I almost made it out the door on time."

"What happened?"

As much as he hated to admit it… "Thought I had enough time to dictate a few of my patients."

"You fell asleep." Not a question.

Widow Serafine shot a curious glance between them. "You need some coffee then, don't you, Dr. Michael?" She didn't give him a chance to answer before she was gesturing to her granddaughter. "Put on the pot, Marie-Louise. We could all do with some waking up."

With a nod, the dark-haired teenager busied herself at the counter. Widow Serafine ushered Michael to a seat at the table. He helped himself to a feast of shrimp, buttery oysters and a rice dish seasoned with bell peppers and green onions.

The great meal made up for the lousy start to the night. He ate while listening to Jillian, Ike, Widow Serafine and the boy Raphael discuss the various tasks to be accomplished to ready the camp for the summer campers. From the conversation, he pieced together the talents the Baptistes brought to the table.

Widow Serafine clearly reigned like a queen over her younger generation, and Michael felt his first hope that Jillian might actually pull off this stunt and survive the first season.

"I'M NOT MAD," Jillian told Michael, not slowing her stride as they made their way back to the camp office.

But that wasn't true. Still, several hours spent with the Baptiste family and Ike, discussing the various jobs to be accomplished during the next few weeks, had alleviated some of her unease about the Baptiste family's unorthodox hiring.

And her concern about running this camp without reliable support from Michael.

"You look mad," he persisted.

Jillian knew he felt guilty for being late. He wanted reassurance but, unfortunately, she was just tired enough, and angry enough, not to give him any. Why should she put forth more effort than he? She'd wanted his help tonight, but he hadn't been available.

"Let's let it go, Michael, please," she said. "It's been a long day for us both. I'm not up to this conversation right now. I have caretakers in place. That's really all that's important."

If the man was smart, he'd cut his losses, but apparently good Creole food had dulled his senses.

"Why didn't you call me?"

Jillian took a deep breath. The rational part of her mind reasoned he only persisted because he felt bad. Michael didn't ever like to let her down—*when* he realized he was letting her down, of course.

But somewhere along the line, their priorities had gotten confused. Their relationship had taken a back seat to dental school, then his practice. Jillian didn't mind caring for the day-to-day things that kept their routine running smoothly. But on the rare occasions she asked for help, she thought Michael should step up to the plate.

Camp Cavelier proved they weren't even playing in the same ball field.

A part of Jillian understood. Michael had devoted himself heart and soul to getting through school and establishing his practice so they could live a comfortable life.

She'd supported him unconditionally because she'd wanted that, too. But they were living a very comfortable life.

So when would their relationship come first?

They'd discussed the situation numerous times, but didn't seem to be managing any changes.

She was beginning to think they never would.

And as Michael walked beside her, waiting expectantly as if he'd deserved *another* reminder to show up tonight, Jillian couldn't help but question how many reminders she was obligated to provide. Two? Four? Why couldn't one be enough?

Along with those questions came a niggling voice in the back of her head, a voice that jogged her memory about all the times she'd reminded him and he'd forgotten anyway.

She'd found a lump in her breast and just last week had gone in for a mammogram. Michael *still* hadn't asked about the outcome. She'd been just busy enough since then, and annoyed enough, not to volunteer the information.

She didn't think he'd ever notice.

"I didn't see the point in calling," she said matter-of-factly. "The clinic phones would be on the answering service, and I knew you wouldn't have your cell phone on."

"You didn't try?"

"No, I didn't."

Such simple words, but his frown told her he heard everything she wasn't saying aloud.

*If my wishes had been important to him, he would have shown up on time without another reminder.*

That truth hung in the air between them, the weight of disappointment so tangible and real. She felt cloaked in that heavy silence.

And righteous.

Michael *should* feel bad. Was what she'd requested of him really so much to ask? He didn't have to ask her to balance his books every day, schedule his appointments, buy birthday gifts for his staff, for his family…. He wouldn't have even remembered his own parents' anniversary had she not stuck a card under his nose and placed a pen in his hand to sign it.

"Don't you think you're being a little unfair, Jillian?"

"Unfair? I told you about this interview a week ago. I mentioned it again at the house this morning. *And* I reminded you before I left the office. How many reminders did you want?"

Emotions played across his handsome face, beginning with a startled hurt and working quickly to anger. He was wrong. He knew it. And he didn't like it.

"Is that why you left your phone in your purse, so I couldn't reach you?" he asked. "Did you want me to worry?"

"Did you worry?"

The exact wrong thing to say. She'd known it as the words had formed in her head, yet she'd let them out anyway.

Michael's expression darkened into a scowl that transformed his face into a stranger's. She'd known her good-natured husband most of her life but always found herself shaken by the heat of his anger when it reared its head, which wasn't often.

They didn't argue.

They discussed. They negotiated. They compromised.

But there didn't seem to be any compromise with Camp Cavalier.

Michael liked to think he was the perfect husband. He always felt bad whenever he didn't live up to his expectations. Unfortunately, she was too angry about his tardiness, and his disinterest in her mammogram appointment—not to mention a host of other things she usually dismissed—to let him feel no guilt. She should have reassured him. Reassurance would have taken so much less energy than this argument.

"Michael, I'm sorry I asked you to come tonight." She didn't make much of an effort to tone down her resignation. "I know it's difficult for you to know exactly when you can get out of the office. I do understand."

But there was no retreat from the road they'd started down. Especially not with such a half-hearted attempt.

"Jillian, the problem isn't me getting out of the office. It's you taking on this camp."

Ouch. He'd made it clear from the start he wasn't gung-ho about the whole idea, yet hearing him toss it out in anger still stung. "I know you had concerns, but I thought you loved this place as much as I do."

"Not enough to run it."

She came to a stop and stared. "It's not as if I've asked you to do a whole lot. You make it sound as if you don't think I can handle it alone."

"Camp Cavelier is a full-time job. You've already got one of those. So do I—a practice and more patients than I know what to do with."

"Now there's the truth. It's a catch-22. We shouldn't work all the time, but you know as well as I do that if we didn't work together, we'd never see each other."

He arched a dark eyebrow in a look that she'd once thought was sexy. Now the expression only cut his point deep. "You don't call running this camp work?"

"Not once we get good people hired and a feel for what needs to be done. I was hoping to renovate Bernice and Carl's cottage. Then we'd have a great weekend getaway. We've wanted one for a while but have been too busy to find one. The camp is the perfect compromise. It's an easy drive from the office. We won't have to maintain the place, or a boat or a stable. All that's already here. Yet, we'll still be able to do all the things we enjoy and don't have time to care for."

"We're caring for the whole damn camp, Jillian. A boat doesn't sound like such a big deal by comparison."

She didn't know why she was trying to sway him to her side, but couldn't seem to stop. "What about our children? Shouldn't we make the effort to preserve history for them? I'd hate for them not to spend their summers at Camp Cavelier."

"What children? We didn't have time to make any even before we bought the camp." He gave a sharp laugh. "But you've solved that problem. You'll have kids swarming all over this place in a few weeks. How many are coming this season—eighty, ninety?"

One hundred and three, but she managed the impulse control not to admit it. Not when Michael was looking all inconvenienced and superior, as if he'd been the one doing all the work around here when he couldn't even make an interview on time.

"I admit this place gets crazy in the summer, but the campers are only here for two months." She tried to interject reason into a subject that didn't feel reasonable tonight. "We still have the rest of the year. Spring and fall are gorgeous. Winter can be, too. Can you imagine celebrating Christmas here?"

"I can imagine celebrating selling this land to a development company and making a fortune. Then you can spend Christmas on that Tahitian island you're always talking about."

"I haven't mentioned visiting a Tahitian island since we were planning our honeymoon. Are you saying you'd actually leave your office long enough to take a vacation?"

He scowled harder and didn't answer.

She scowled right back. Of all the low blows…

"I can't believe you'd even bring up developing this land. You know I promised Bernice and Carl. That was the whole reason they sold it to me for the price they did."

"There's nothing in the contract prohibiting us—"

"It was a verbal agreement I took seriously. Bernice and Carl trusted us to bring the camp into the twenty-first century. They had enough heartache losing their only son in the Vietnam War. Doesn't trust mean anything to you?"

Her reminder fell flat between them. She could see Michael trying to rein in his anger, recognized how much effort it took, effort that felt as hurtful as his whole uncaring attitude.

What did he have to feel angry about?

She hadn't asked anything of him except for a little support. She'd honestly thought he'd come through. And not the half-hearted, whenever-it's-convenient efforts he'd been making. Not when she'd always done her one-hundred-and-ten-percent best to support everything he'd ever wanted.

Why else would she have given up a full ride to Duke if not to accompany him to college?

Why would she have crammed her course load into half the time if not to accompany him to dental school?

Why would she have turned down so many job opportunities if not to start up his practice?

Folding her arms over her chest as if that would help her keep her mouth shut, Jillian glared at him.

"Camp Cavelier is a life calling, not a hobby," Michael said through clenched teeth. "Look at the Virgils. Look at Ike. Unless you want to close my practice and relocate here to do this job right then developing this land only makes sense. Bernice and Carl couldn't find anyone to buy the place because it's a lot of damn work."

"That's why I hired caretakers." She shoved the words through teeth as tightly clenched. "We chose to return to Natchez to start up your practice and rear our family, so shouldn't we be willing to put some effort into steering Natchez into the future? Life might be a little hectic for a while, Michael, but how is that any different than it's ever been to reach our goals?"

"*Your* goal, you mean."

That's what the whole situation really all boiled down to—Michael was only interested in what *he* wanted.

The realization felt like a slap in the face, when she supposed it shouldn't. Suddenly, she could see the emerging pattern so clearly.

She lived with him, worked with him, slept with him— it had always been about *him*. Ever since they were young, their lives had always been about what Michael wanted.

Michael, Michael, *Michael!*

She'd always gone along because she knew successful couples didn't argue—they negotiated and compromised.

Jillian was getting tired of compromising.

"You know, Michael, that's the real problem here. Life

is fine as long as you get what you want, but the second you have to return the favor, you can't be counted on."

"That's not fair—"

"I don't know why I've let this be okay for so long, but this isn't fair. I refuse to be married to a man who only thinks about himself."

Now it was Michael's turn to reel as if he'd been slapped, and mingled with her horror over what had degenerated into a nasty fight was satisfaction that she'd shocked him.

It was an unfamiliar, *ugly* feeling.

"What the hell does that mean?" he demanded.

"It means I'm too upset to continue *this*. We need to table this conversation until we've both had a chance to think about how we want to handle this."

Because if she didn't get in the car and have time to cool off on the drive home, she was going to say something that would end her marriage right here and now.

"YOU'RE EAVESDROPPING, Widow," Raphael announced as he stepped through the cottage door to find Serafine sitting in the porch swing, rocking herself to the music of the rushing river.

Back home in Bayou Doré the nights were already sultry and hot, even after the sun went down. Here in Mississippi, darkness cooled the air, and the Landrys' voices carried on the breeze.

"Need to test the water around here, don't you think?"

"The Landrys seemed like nice enough people until you got them arguing."

"That argument's been brewing a lot longer than I been in Natchez," Serafine scoffed. "Y'know, boy, I've got a really good feeling about this place. I knew as soon I read Mrs. Jillian's advertisement we were meant to be here. Didn't question it for a second. I just wasn't sure why. I mean I knew the obvious—this job is a perfect fit for you and your kin, but there was more."

"Don't be meddling with these people."

The warning in Raphael's voice made her smile. He didn't quite come out and argue, and that show of respect—however slight—marked a self-discipline she was happy to see finally in this young man.

"Haven't been here long enough to be meddling with anyone, I just said."

"You bullied Mrs. Jillian into giving us these jobs. You made her feel guilty, and she was nice enough to let you."

"Ah, Raphael. You know how it is. I *know* we're here for a purpose. Just have to figure out what it is, and how to do the job. Can't get about business if Mrs. Jillian kept with her ideas about interviews and reference-checking. Why should we waste time when Mrs. Jillian only needed a bit of convincing?"

"I'd say you've been here long enough to meddle."

"I'm only moving things along in the direction they're meant to be moving. Your granny had the gift of *knowing* even stronger than I do. And Marie-Louise, too, even though you tell her to keep her feelings to herself."

"My granny didn't take with your hoodoo ways, Widow. You know that."

"Your granny couldn't deny who she was no matter how far and fast she ran from the bayou. She finally accepted it, too. Why do you think she sent you back to the family for rearing when she passed?"

Raphael frowned, an expression that bore so much responsibility for a boy who should have been exploring his youth with laughter. She wished he could bridge the distance between pride and his rejection of their family.

"For the record, I don't practice hoodoo. I'm a God-fearing woman through and through. Just like the rest of your family."

Baptistes were Baptistes were Baptistes. Life would be simpler all the way around if Virginie's brood would accept they had people who cared for them. If they'd make an effort to fit in and accept a little help and guidance, they might just stand a chance of making something of their lives. That's exactly what her baby sister had wanted, Serafine knew.

Virginie had known her eldest sister would feel obligated to do right by these kids, whether she'd admitted the truth to Raphael or not. There'd been bad blood between Serafine and her baby sister. Not intentional, of course. Serafine hadn't wanted to marry Virginie's beloved no more than Virginie had wanted to fall in love with the dashing politician from New Iberia Parish.

Neither sister had had a choice.

Not Serafine, whose daddy had decreed his eldest daughter should marry the boy he thought destined to become the next Louisiana governor.

Not Virginie, who'd been in love with falling in love and had used the whole situation as an excuse to break free of the bayou with the next rogue who'd sailed through their swamp.

Serafine had stood by her man's side until the day he died, not because she'd loved Laurent Mercier but because that had been her duty.

Once she'd pressed her lips to the cool granite of his tomb, her duty had been done. She'd adopted the sobriquet of *Widow,* stepped into her husband's place to rule their brood and refused to marry again.

This time her daddy hadn't insisted otherwise.

He'd left Serafine free to do what she did best—set people to rights. And here she was in Natchez, doing just that. She'd thought only Virginie's brood needed setting, but after eavesdropping on the Landrys, she *knew* more than three young 'uns needed her help.

She only wished Raphael would accept the situation so easily, and if his scowl was any indication…

"If you're going to meddle, maybe me and my kin should keep moving on to Shreveport," he said grimly. "Marie-Louise will turn eighteen soon."

The reminder irked Serafine. Raphael and Philip had only stayed in Bayou Doré because they wouldn't leave their sister behind. Once Marie-Louise reached the age of majority, the girl could make her own choices. No question she'd follow her brothers wherever they wanted to go.

"What are you planning to do in Shreveport, boy? Keep working on your jobs that take from sunup to sundown and barely pay the bills? You want a better life for your kin, but with you working so hard, you can't keep your eyes on them. Philip's already running wild, and Marie-Louise hasn't turned up with a big belly yet because she's holding out for true love—like your granny did. Better hope true love doesn't turn out to be a scoundrel like your grand-daddy. He spirited my baby sister from the bayou with his smooth talk and pretty smiles then left her breeding and too proud to come home."

Raphael speared his fingers through his hair. To the boy's credit, he didn't deny her claims, though Serafine *knew* he wanted to. But Raphael had been privy to that part of his grandparents' history, at least. He'd been reared without parents for the very same reason and was smart enough to know that, left to run wild, Philip and Marie-Louise would get themselves into trouble.

"You're their only hope and you know it," Serafine pointed out. "They listen to you. Your fortune's going to change in Natchez, boy. I *feel* it. We're here for a reason, and if you're smart, you'll keep that chip on your shoulder under your collar. For your kin's sake. Your own, too."

Raphael narrowed his gaze, but Serafine only clapped a hand on his back and smiled.

"Like it or not, boy, I love you and your kin. You remind me of my baby sister. I lost too many years with her. I plan to make the most of what I can get with you. You hear me?"

"I hear you, Widow."

"Good. Then you might try working with me instead of against me for a change. Together, we might work some magic around here."

Raphael met her gaze with those eyes that saw so much more than she'd wanted to reveal, a look that was pure Virginie. "That's what I'm afraid of. That's *exactly* what I'm afraid of."

But not all magic was hoodoo. Not all magic need be feared. A lesson Raphael was about to learn.

# 3

*Several days later*

"JILLIAN." Charlotte poked her head through the open office door. "I've got a woman in the reception area who doesn't have an appointment, but says you'll squeeze her in. Do you know a Serafine Baptiste-Mercier?"

Jillian nodded and rolled the chair away from the desk. "Why does she need an appointment?"

"Broken bridge."

Darn. This was the absolute last thing that needed to happen right now. As was typical, the clinic was busy, but worse than that, there was an oppressive tension in the air. Primarily because she and Michael weren't right. She was still angry—at him for being so selfish and at herself for placing the status of their marriage in question.

There was a reason she didn't like to argue, and Jillian had remembered it—somewhere between the drive back from camp the other night and the drive to work the following morning. Arguments fueled hurt feelings and fighting words—and statements made in anger affected everything and proved hard to take back.

But for now, she had to wedge another appointment

into a crammed schedule. What else could she do about Widow Serafine—tell her brand-new caretaker to find another dentist?

With a sigh, Jillian glanced at the computer monitor. "Michael did book some extra time this afternoon to get that temporary crown out of his mouth. He might be able to squeeze her in."

"Glad you mentioned it. I assume he's expecting me to put his new crown in."

Jillian recognized a rhetorical question and didn't bother with a reply.

"So who's this woman?"

"Widow Serafine, my new camp caretaker. She's only been in town a few days."

"Why do you look so stressed? You know Michael will take care of her."

"I know." She must have sounded as indecisive as she felt because Charlotte eyed her narrowly.

"I knew it. You two have been parading around here all week like strangers. Why haven't you patched things up yet, Jillian?"

"It was a pretty nasty argument."

"You're going to make me stressed if you don't get this thing all settled. You're my favorite couple, you know?"

Jillian shrugged, not sure what to say. Some things just weren't a quick fix. This situation had risen like the river during a hurricane. Up and over the levee then right through their lives.

"Well, I'm no marriage counselor, but I'm here if you want someone to listen," Charlotte said. "Now you better go deal with your new caretaker. She's a character, that's for sure. I left her chatting it up with the Baker twins."

"Oh, my."

The Baker twins were the owners of an antebellum house that sat majestically on the bluff overlooking Natchez Under-the-Hill. Descended from a family that had grown wealthy during the cotton boom of the early nineteenth century, the Baker twins considered themselves Natchez royalty.

They lived in the upper stories of their family home and had opened the lower to the public. A cherished stop on the National Register tour, the Baker family home gave guests the opportunity to explore the nearby historic district. Under-the-Hill offered carriage rides with coachmen who could talk about the Cotton Kingdom origins and steamboat traffic as if they'd lived the lives of wealthy plantation owners.

As far as Jillian knew, these two eccentric old ladies didn't talk to anyone but each other, their tour guests and their fourteen cats. They'd deigned to grace Michael with their business only after failing eyesight had finally forced Dr. Cavanaugh, the town's long-time dentist, into retirement.

Following Charlotte toward the reception area, Jillian noted that Michael was inside exam room two, complimenting his young patient on her oral hygiene after her first month in braces. He didn't look up as she passed.

Neither did Widow Serafine. But Jillian did a double take in the doorway of the reception area when she found her caretaker had actually sandwiched herself between the Baker twins on the leather sofa. Eugenie and Eulalie looked more than a bit shell-shocked with this striking stranger between them.

The scene could have been a skit from *Comedy Central.* The two wispy old ladies in their impeccable vintage dresses looked on the verge of swooning. By comparison Widow Serafine could have blown in on a hurricane squall. Not only did she equal the size of both Baker sisters combined, but her ensemble was as bright as a carnival tent.

After asking and answering her own question, Widow Serafine's laughter rang out, too big for what Jillian had always considered a spacious and comfortable waiting room.

The Baker twins clearly didn't know what to make of their new acquaintance, so Jillian jumped to the rescue.

"Widow Serafine, I see you've met Natchez's ladies of distinction. Eugenie and Eulalie Baker own that gorgeous antebellum house on the bluff. They're an important part of our heritage around here." She hoped a deferential introduction would shake the twins from their daze and smooth any ruffled feathers. "Ladies, Widow Serafine is the new caretaker at Camp Cavelier. She's newly arrived from New Orleans with her family."

Two identical watery blue gazes focused in a disbelieving look that anyone would actually invite this woman to town. Jillian shut down any further conversation by reassuring the twins that Charlotte would retrieve them shortly.

"You can come with me, so I can get some information," she told Widow Serafine, who swept past in a cloud of inviting lavender scent.

"I can't tell you how much I appreciate you fitting me in today." She smiled a crooked smile to reveal the empty space where two upper molars should have been. "I couldn't believe the luck. Marie-Louise and I were scrubbing out the shower stalls in the girls' cabins when the darn thing broke clean in two. Had it been any smaller, I'd have swallowed it."

She extended a hand to reveal the offending bit of dentistry, which was exactly in the condition she claimed.

"I'm sure Michael won't have any trouble repairing it." Settling Widow Serafine into her office guest chair, Jillian learned that she was the one in for trouble after asking for a dental insurance card.

"Dental coverage is one of the perks that comes with the caretaker job, isn't it?" Widow Serafine asked.

"Yes, it is."

"And when does that coverage kick in?"

"Ninety days."

Widow Serafine placed the broken bridge on the desk and eyed the dislodged teeth with a contemplative expression. "I suppose I can come back then."

"You don't have any dental coverage?"

"Not since my husband died. God bless his soul. The government doesn't keep providing for his widow, and those monthly payments were more than my mortgage. Wish I didn't have to keep paying for a house that's been blown away, truth be told." Widow Serafine beamed a smile that revealed her missing molars. "Think you could hang on to the bill for ninety days until the coverage kicks in?"

Not unless she wanted to perpetrate insurance fraud. Jillian kept that to herself, but for a woman who normally handled her husband's business efficiently, she found herself back to being speechless again.

Which gave Widow Serafine the upper hand.

"Back home old Doc Roup lets my kin work off my bill," she explained. "My boy Denis is a carpenter. He fixes up whatever Doc needs fixing. My girl Lucie trims his hair—well, what little he has left, anyway. If I just need a filling, Doc'll settle up for a big pot of my gumbo. Or bouillabaisse when Lucie's husband goes out fishing. Says I make the best bouillabaisse in the whole parish. And I do, Mrs. Jillian. Do you like bouillabaisse?"

Jillian wondered what it was about this woman that kept catching her off guard. She ran into her fair share of characters around here. Michael was well-loved in town, which translated into a patient base of diverse demography— from eccentric old-timers like the Baker twins to members of local law-enforcement agencies and philanthropists like Amelia Preston.

Jillian knew Michael wouldn't think twice about accepting a pot of whatever the widow might be cooking as repayment for her bridge. But this wasn't exactly the best of times to be asking him for a freebie connected to Camp Cavelier.

But as she saw Widow Serafine's newly imperfect smile reflected in her dark eyes, Jillian didn't have a choice. She wouldn't suggest the woman make the nearly four-hour drive to visit old Doc Roup. Nor did she feel right about taking the widow up on her suggestion to walk around without her bridge until her dental coverage kicked in.

No, the only way Jillian could look herself in the mirror meant forcing a smile and saying, "Actually, I think the office staff might enjoy a pot of gumbo for lunch one day."

"BITE DOWN," Michael said.

Widow Serafine did as he asked, and he inspected the impression, pleased with a job well done.

"There you go. Good as new."

He stripped off sanitary gloves while Charlotte unfastened the paper bib from around Widow Serafine's neck.

"You're a miracle worker, Dr. Michael," the widow said as he shifted the dental chair into an upright position.

Michael smiled, appreciating the sentiment even if he hadn't exactly earned such accolades. The repair job had been simple.

"Now, you're sure I didn't run you too far off your schedule?" Widow Serafine asked. "You got plenty of time to get that crown of yours in your own mouth, right?"

She pointed to the equipment shelf behind him, and Michael followed her gaze to the bit of porcelain residing there. "Not a problem. In fact, Charlotte will put it in right now just so we don't forget."

"Thanks for telling me." Charlotte snapped a glove on her hand with ceremony.

"Then I'll get home to planning the menu. You sure you don't want your luncheon until Monday?"

"Can't think of a better way to start a week around here," he said.

Charlotte nodded. "Now there's a truth."

"Just remember," he told Widow Serafine as she swung her legs out of the chair and took his hand for a gentlemanly assist. "Go easy on that bridge until dinner. After that you can eat normally."

"You betcha, Dr. Michael. Thanks again."

"My pleasure." He smiled as Widow Serafine disappeared down the hallway. Then he took his place in the dental chair.

Charlotte prepared the cement, and the process of replacing his temporary with a new crown took all of five minutes. He tested the impression and declared his bite satisfactory.

"You do good work." He smiled widely, one of the cheesy smiles he coaxed out of his patients to capture on film and grace his office walls.

"Of course I do," Charlotte said. "Now get back to work before we wind up working straight through lunch."

But Michael hadn't yet left the exam room to greet his next patient when Jillian showed up. He bit back a casual greeting—her serious expression told him everything he needed to know about her mood.

Damn it. Was she ever going to let their argument go, or was she planning to hold a grudge forever?

Or had she expected him to take her threats about their marriage seriously?

*Right.*

He eyed her chilly expression and settled on a noncommittal, "What's up?"

"Did you get your crown in?"

"Good as new."

"I just wanted to thank you for squeezing in Widow Serafine this morning."

"No problem." He glanced at his watch. "Should still have time to finish up, eat lunch and take a quick nap."

"I'm glad," she said. "Wouldn't want you to miss your beauty rest."

Michael glanced up, but Jillian had already turned and headed out the door.

His beauty rest?

He frowned at her retreating back. Widow Serafine might not technically have been his patient before today, but the woman had needed her bridge repaired. Had Jillian honestly expected him to turn her away?

No, which meant she was still holding a major grudge about Camp Cavelier.

Michael knew the drill. Because he'd run late for the interview and because of the things he'd said in the heat of the moment, so she'd decided to interpret his reservations about the camp to mean he didn't want to be involved. He didn't, of course, but he would never abandon her on one of her crusades.

He'd apologized, but, unfortunately, it looked like an apology wasn't going to do the trick. Jillian was too damned efficient and proud. She didn't like needing help in the best of circumstances. In all the years he'd known her, he couldn't ever remember hearing her admit she'd bitten off more than she could chew. And she had, a few times.

His incredibly competent wife routinely faced challenges that would send most people running in the opposite direction. She always managed to buck up and keep her eyes on the goal, though. He knew the craziness would eventually pass, the pressure would be off and their days would return to normal.

But life could get hairy in the process....

On the rare occasions Michael had run afoul of her efforts, he'd found himself eliminated from the equation. Camp business, including Widow Serafine and her family, would now become Jillian's exclusive domain.

He frowned at the doorway.

His beauty rest?

Her pettiness surprised him. Until right now, he hadn't even known she could be petty.

While working on his next patient, Michael considered what he might do to ease his way back into her good graces. Not that he had any burning desire to squeeze more work into his already overbooked days. But Jillian's mood was translating into every aspect of their lives. She was freezing him out, and he didn't relish a summer with her ignoring him because she was mad.

Should he send flowers? She loved gladioli, and he couldn't remember the last time he'd brought her any. An anniversary maybe? But which one?

What about candy? She had a sweet tooth, and a box of expensive chocolate—milk, not dark—might assuage her temper.

Michael debated flowers versus chocolate as he wrapped up his morning, inhaled his lunch then settled into his office easy chair for a turbo nap.

By the time he'd awakened, refreshed and ready to take on the afternoon, he'd decided on the flowers. Had Jillian mentioned watching her weight lately? He couldn't remember, but didn't want to seem unsupportive of her efforts if she was.

Flowers would definitely be safer.

But Jillian was angrier than he'd ever seen her. Maybe he should take her to dinner. Hmm. That idea had potential. Dinner would mean she wouldn't have to cook. If he presented his invitation right, not only would he seem sensitive, but unselfish because he hated leaving the house once he'd settled in after a long day.

Yeah, Jillian might really like dinner.

So after he finished his last patient of the day, Michael planned his strategy. She'd driven her own car into work, so he arrived home behind her, moved quietly through the house and caught up with her in the bathroom as she stripped off her uniform.

With the smock coming over her head, she didn't see him sneak up behind her, but he got an eyeful. Strawberry-blond waves tumbled down her back as she deposited the shirt into the hamper. She wore a white cotton bra that looked so sexy.

Trailing his gaze down to the curvy V of her waist, he imagined slipping his arms around her, unfastening the clasp and trying a few moves sure to coax out those soft sighs she made whenever he touched her.

Maybe she'd be so taken by his thoughtfulness that he'd luck out and score. After a good meal, Michael would get a second wind. How long had it been since they'd made love anyway?

"Hey, gorgeous." He caught her around the waist.

She let out a surprised yelp then went stiff in his arms. *Not good.*

Twisting her around, he gazed down into her face. "Surprised to see me?"

"I didn't hear you come in."

"What do you say about dinner at Kevin's tonight? Let me make up for being such an ass about the interview. We can discuss the camp. What do you say?"

She said nothing at all, just eyed him through a narrowed gaze as if she wasn't sure whether or not to believe him.

It was enough to hurt a guy's pride. "I don't want you angry with me anymore. And I don't want you thinking about not being married to me, either." He nuzzled his cheek against the top of her head.

"Finally got your attention, did I?"

"Of course you got my attention." He squelched a wave of irritation and forced his tone to remain conciliatory. "Let's fix things. We don't stay angry at each other. That's what other couples do, not us."

She still didn't reply, so he tried again.

"Come on, Jilly." He coaxed. "Kevin owes me for missing his last appointment. I'm sure he'll give us a last-minute table. We love going to Kevin's. It's our special place."

Would she give him a chance to make peace so they could get past this or would she keep hanging on to her anger?

She frowned, considering, but didn't pull away. He considered that a good sign.

He tried again. "I don't want you to have to cook. Not even to reheat last night's leftovers. You've had a busy day. I want you to relax and be waited on tonight."

"You don't like going out after you get home from work."

Okay, she was talking to him. That was a step in the right direction.

"Doesn't matter what I like. I'm trying to apologize here."

His words hung in the air between them, and he could feel her indecision in the way she'd started relaxing against him.

He went in for the kill. "I'm groveling, Jilly. Come on. Let me fix this."

"You think dinner's going to do that?"

"It's a start. We'll discuss the camp. I'm sure we can come up with something. We always do."

He tightened his grip until she came up close against him, all her curves touching him in exactly the right places, sparking life signs just as she always did. "I want you to know how much I appreciate you and everything you do for me."

"I'm your wife and office manager. I'm doing my jobs."

"Which I don't tell you often enough how much I appreciate."

"I know you do."

Tipping her head back, she gazed up into his face, the distance in her eyes beginning to melt away. She slipped her arms around his waist and rested her head on his shoulder.

*First base.*

"You don't think it's kind of late for dinner?" she asked.

"If we get a move on, we could probably be seated by seven-thirty."

"It'll be after eight by the time we're served."

Michael knew what was happening here, and if he didn't catch her quickly, she'd talk herself out of his thoughtful gesture. "I wanted to do something nice so you know how much I appreciate the way you handle my patients."

"Especially when you get behind?"

"Most especially when I get behind."

"I owed you. For taking care of Widow Serafine."

She was testing him, mentioning the camp to see how he responded. He walked a razor-sharp line with his response and shot for the right mix of repentant and sincere. Any defense would only lose the ground he'd gained.

"Widow Serafine is our caretaker. If we take good care of her, she'll take good care of us, don't you think?"

Again, she peered at him as if deciding whether or not to take him seriously.

"You know me, Jillian. Mr. Sweet Guy. That's why you married me, remember? I'd never leave a lady without her teeth."

The second it was out of his mouth, Michael knew it had

been exactly the right thing to say. He could feel the last of her resistance melt away as she relaxed against him.

*Second base.*

He didn't pressure her with words, just rested his chin on the top of her head, inhaling the scent of her, always fresh and feminine, not perfumed but reminding him of the way the air smelled after a spring rain.

He could see their reflections in the vanity mirror. Jillian looked sexy with so much bare skin revealed, her arms relaxed as she held him around the waist. He liked the way they looked together, *right,* the long lines of her body molding against him to create the perfect fit.

"He wants sex."

"I always want sex with you." He dropped his voice an octave into what Jillian always called his bedroom voice. "If you think it's too late, we can always skip dinner and go straight for dessert."

That statement didn't have quite the effect he'd expected.

Jillian exhaled heavily. "At least it won't be the kind of dessert that'll put on any weight."

He'd made a good call on the chocolate. Crowding her against the wall, Michael gave in to the urge to remove her bra.

"Michael, what are you—" Jillian broke off her words on a sigh when he filled his hands with her warm skin.

He recognized the mixture of hesitation and yearning in her voice, a tone that always made his blood crash straight to his crotch. Her mind might be saying, "No, we really shouldn't." But her body was saying, "Take me, I'm yours."

He thumbed her nipples, a deep slow stroke, and was rewarded when the tips speared into tight peaks. She arched just enough to invite him to further exploration, and he found the sight of her reflection arousing in the extreme.

His hands looked dark against her skin, and she was all beautiful curves as she leaned her head against the wall, exposing the graceful sweep of her neck. Michael couldn't have resisted a taste if his life had depended on it.

Lowering his mouth to the pulse beating low in her throat, he pressed an open-mouthed kiss there.

Jillian shivered.

He sucked gently, and was rewarded when she inhaled a long breath that whispered brokenly against his hair. He couldn't resist dragging his hands down her ribs and anchoring her closer. He rode his growing erection against her belly. She rocked her hips, making him swell so hard his pants seam bit painfully into his skin, which dampened his enthusiasm for foreplay in the bathroom. Disentangling himself, he caught her around the waist and under her knees then lifted her into his arms.

She draped her arms around his neck to hang on. "You're going to hurt your back."

Michael only laughed, a sound that burst out harder than he'd intended and made her scowl knowingly.

Okay, so he wasn't as young as he'd once been... "I can still think of a few ways to show my appreciation, Jilly."

She turned to gaze in the mirror. "That's not the problem. I've been watching what I eat, but I think my metabolism is slowing down now that I'm thirty."

Michael exhaled a snort of disbelief that managed *not* to sound as if he was gasping for air. Maneuvering her through the bathroom doorway, he deposited her on the side of the bed. He didn't give her a chance to protest, or to get away. Catching her around the waist, he worked the jumble of uniform and cotton panties down her legs before tossing the whole thing onto the floor.

He raked his gaze down the length of her, as gorgeous now as the first time he'd set eyes on her. He could still remember the day he'd been treated to seeing Jillian completely nude, after a good year's worth of glimpsing tantalizing bits and pieces during some heavy make-out sessions.

But the night they'd skinny-dipped in Lake Lily…

*Jillian peeled away her jeans and stood clad only in a flannel shirt that barely reached the tops of her thighs. She was all slim curves and long legs, and Michael knew she wasn't wearing a bra because he'd copped a feel earlier. His heartbeat came to a crashing stop as she lifted her arms….*

*He could see the barest hint of her heart-shaped bottom below the hem of the shirt…sleek thighs that would be soft to his touch. He wanted her so badly right then that his whole body became a furnace of need, every muscle so tight it ached, his skin so hot that by rights he should have melted.*

*Then she lifted the shirt away. His heartbeat kicked in violently, thudding so hard it might explode out of his chest. Of course, he could only see her from behind, but he'd never seen a sight more beautiful in his life.*

*Her skin gleamed pale in the moonlight that made her hair look almost silver. He drank in the sight of her, his own reaction raging so wildly out of control that he had to brace himself against a tree to keep standing.*

*She hadn't yet turned around, and he guessed she was feeling shy. He felt his nudity in a way he never had before, but didn't have the brain cells to dwell on the feeling because his dick had gotten so hard he thought it might explode, too.*

To this day Jillian was the most beautiful woman Michael had ever seen. He liked the way she looked stretched across their bed, wearing only her tousled hair and white socks. Nowadays, she trimmed the curls between her thighs until there wasn't much more than a hint of reddish-blond to tempt him. She claimed to be keeping neat for swimsuit season, but he guessed she could feel his mouth better when he went down on her.

That thought drove him to his knees.

Grabbing her ankles, he pulled her toward the edge of the bed. She laughed as her bottom scooted over the comforter, and her thighs fell apart in welcome.

He settled in comfortably then lowered his face to her warm skin. She tasted familiar and inviting, her every sigh rushing him with the push of a tide.

"Oh, Michael. You've got such a gift."

He chuckled at that, a burst of warm breath that made her thighs quiver.

Determined to wipe away the fallout from their dispute about the camp, Michael pulled out every trick in his arsenal. He wanted reality to disappear beneath the pleasure of sensation. He'd had the benefit of years to hone these skills. He knew how to arouse her.

Easing his hands up the smooth expanse of her belly, he teased her breasts until she squirmed against him. She had always melted beneath his touch, her body responding so completely he knew they'd been made for each other.

Her pleasure was his pleasure, and Michael knew no greater contentment than commanding her responses, no greater arousal. Those sighs tested his restraint every damn time.

When she began rocking her hips, trying to knead her orgasm into breaking, she was all his. Redoubling his efforts, he took her apart in a way he hoped would soften her mood when she came back down to earth. When she came apart, she dissolved into a puddle of pulsing softness and quivering skin that made him ache.

Resting his face against her thigh, he breathed deeply, managing the ache in his crotch that demanded equal time. But Jillian knew. She'd always been one to give as good as she got. Before he knew it, she was reaching for him, their hands and arms tangling as they divested him of his clothes.

He finally sank onto the bed beside her. He went to pull her into his arms, but Jillian only laughed and dodged him. She slithered down the length of his body in a gut-tightening burst of warm skin and muscle, and burrowed herself between his legs.

"One good turn and all that…"

Michael wasn't about to look a gift blow-job in the face, and enjoyed a moment of satisfaction for his own job well done.

Jillian could have been a pin-up girl with her red-gold waves tumbling over his thighs, bare curves covering the terrain of the bed in a mouth-watering display. Michael relaxed into the pillows to savor the view, but relaxation didn't last before Jillian zeroed in on her target.

Slipping her warm fingers around his erection, she gave a light tug that brought him up off the bed. His body went from zero to sixty, his hot skin surging into her grip with an enthusiasm that made her smile. He had the absent thought that while his back might be showing the effects of age, his body still responded to her as it had when they'd been younger.

She toyed with him, idly stroking as she settled in. Then, propped on an elbow, she lowered her face for that first taste.

Michael had expected her to ease into pleasure, but she surprised him. She sucked him down whole, a lip-lock that crushed the breath from his lungs. Every muscle in his body gathered in response to that sucking pull, and she drew lightly again and again. He closed his eyes and gave himself over to her, utterly content with the turn this night had taken.

Time slowed to a haze of erotic awareness…her wet mouth on his skin…her firm grip working him in lazy time…the tension inside coiling until he could only ride each stroke…fingers threading into her hair, touching an anchor as his ass came off the bed as she worked him knowingly.

"My neck is about to break."

Michael opened his eyes. He found Jillian exactly where he'd left her—wedged between his legs with her mouth wrapped around him. Yet her discomfort had yanked him from his dreamy daze. He didn't want to hurt her and was about to suggest a change of position…

"Maybe if I bend my head his way… There, that's better. Now I'm not rebounding off his stomach."

The hairs raised along his skin as he stared at her shifting her shoulders so she stopped *rebounding off his stomach*. Some barely functioning part of his brain registered that while he'd heard her speak, he hadn't actually seen her. From where he was, her mouth looked totally occupied, working him with that steady, knee-melting motion.

He was too passion-dazed to figure out what was bugging him about that, so he just watched as she stepped up her pace, sucking him in so far that he was sure she would choke.

But, as usual, Jillian was in control. His body reacted instinctively, his thighs shaking, and he managed to keep his eyes open and his gaze on her face when she said, "I know what'll make him get this show on the road."

She slithered her fingers beneath his balls.

And as raw sensation and the vestiges of his reason collided, he finally pulled together what was happening.

Michael wasn't hearing what Jillian was saying because she wasn't talking.

As impossible as it might seem, he had to be hearing what she was *thinking*.

# 4

JILLIAN would have been content with bringing Michael to orgasm then falling asleep. Her body felt sated and heavy from her own satisfaction, and she wanted just to forget the ugliness of the past few days, get a break from the resentment she'd been feeling toward him. A few extra hours of sleep tonight wouldn't kill her, either.

But just as she had him on the brink, she sensed him holding back. She suspected he meant to prolong their sexy encounter as a way of showing his appreciation. And here she'd been trying to bring him satisfaction *quickly*.

Pre Camp Cavalier, she'd have welcomed the possibility of a second orgasm. But today had been a long day in an otherwise unpleasant week, and she felt a mild sense of disappointment that she couldn't give in to this dreamy sense of contentment.

When she was this tired, lying down always proved the kiss of death. Her orgasm already had her on the verge of a coma. But Michael was trying so hard to make things right again between them. How could she do any less?

But she'd need to find a second wind to get excited about making love.

She managed to rally a show of enthusiasm when

Michael reached for her and pulled her into his arms. With her help, he maneuvered them beneath the bedding then held her close, as if savoring the feel of their bodies molding against each other in the shelter of their bed.

The moment felt drowsy and tender with him all warm and hard against her, his arms gripping her tight, his erection cradled against her stomach, proving that he wanted her as much as he always had. If she tried really hard, she could forget the unpleasantness of their argument and remember the days when they'd been young lovers who'd blown off the whole world to spend long days exploring each other with passion and enthusiasm.

The memory of all that long-ago lust was enough to make her smile. Tipping her face to his, she captured his mouth in a kiss. His lips yielded easily beneath hers. He tightened his arms around her, until she could feel the press of his body everywhere. He was such a wonderful kisser, and they lay facing each other, snug in the cocoon of their bed, hands roaming lazily over bare skin, enjoying a leisurely exploration of contented bodies, twining tongues and shared breaths.

Jillian would have been content simply to lie here forever, but Michael's erection presented an only faintly diminished reminder that just one of them had been satisfied.

Unfortunately, as much as she enjoyed the feel of his strong hands rounding the trail of her waist and hip, she wasn't experiencing anything that even resembled a life sign. Her wonderful orgasm had used up her limited supply of energy, and she needed a bit of an assist to get moving.

With a sigh, she brought her hands up to his face and forced more eagerness into her kiss. She pressed closer against him, nudging her knee between his until his hard thigh pressed against her sensitive places. She focused her wandering thoughts on the familiar feel of his body.

Dragging her open hands down the length of his back, she traced the nicely rounded butt that had once been the envy of all the girls on her high-school cheerleading squad. During Michael's senior year, he'd been firmly ensconced as the football hero, and not a game passed when one or the other of her fellow cheerleaders wouldn't mess up a cheer because she was too busy staring at the star quarterback's backside.

Jillian had been a lowly sophomore at the time, and so proud to have been Michael's girlfriend. Fourteen years later, and she was still proud to be with him, even if his butt wasn't as tight. Sinking her fingers into his cheeks, she pictured him as he'd been during their college years, when he'd still been playing football while carrying a full course load, a dashing young student who could make love to her for hours on end.

She could almost feel him as he'd been then, taut and hard, filled with that restless energy of youth. She inhaled the never-changing scent of him, all husky, all male, all Michael. She tasted his mouth, his smile wide and perfect. His kiss tonight wasn't as demanding as she knew he could be…which wasn't going to work. If Jillian expected to stay awake, she'd have to wake Michael up, too.

Sliding her hands between them, she stroked his fading erection, thrilled when he surged easily to life again, his length growing beneath her caresses, promising her more of those yummy orgasms.

Closing her eyes, she narrowed her senses to the way

he felt in her palms, the pulse that made his erection throb with every beat of his heart.

Suddenly, in her mind's eye, Jillian could see him as he'd been a few years back…after college, but before their lifestyle and his practice had precluded the time for regular workouts. His smile was fast and charming, his butt tight. She conjured the image of him as a bad boy, wearing low-slung jeans and a worn leather jacket. Stylish sunglasses over stubbled cheeks, and a pack of cigarettes visible in his pocket.

*Mmm.* He looked so good, and the first twinge of awareness cut through the drowsy haze that held her in its grip.

Jillian broke their kiss and trailed her mouth along his jaw and down his throat, pressing open-mouthed kisses to his skin that placed the taste of him on her tongue and encouraged her imagination to gain speed.

Her fantasy involved the image of a leather-clad Michael in her mind and the question of how she, nice girl from nice family that she was, could have encountered such a bad boy.

Jillian decided that she would have met him purely by chance. Perhaps she strolled out of the salon on Main Street one night after work and he'd been standing there in full bad-boy mode, arms folded across his broad chest, leaning against his motorcycle—a sweet polished black chopper with neon purple underglow illuminating the chassis…

*What he was doing there, Jillian didn't know, or care. The only thing she cared about was the look in his eyes as he raked his gaze from the top of her newly styled hair down the terrain of her body to her bare legs and strappy sandals that revealed her fresh pedicure.*

With the illogic of dreams and fantasies, apparently, he wore leather while she wore a sundress, remarkably similar

to the one Marie-Louise had been wearing the night they'd
met, a floral print that was lightweight and feminine and
molded Jillian's curves with stylish precision.

*His blue eyes swallowed the sight of her whole, made her
feel empowered by the approval that he didn't bother to hide.*

*"Hop on, gorgeous. If you dare." His voice was throaty
and low, filled with challenge. As if he'd pegged her for a nice
girl who wouldn't dare to associate with anyone like him.*

*Jillian's reason shrieked that he was exactly the kind of
temptation Pastor Crowley had been warning against in
every sermon he'd ever delivered from the pulpit. But she
knew bad-boy Michael would take her for a ride on the wild
side that she'd never forget.*

*He must have read the answer in her eyes because he
slid into the saddle and extended a hand.*

*Jillian was forced to hike her dress high to slip onto the
seat behind him. His gaze caught and held on the expanse
of pale thigh and his eyes twinkled as she settled against
him, slipping her arms around his waist, her thighs
molding his tight butt.*

*He glanced back over his shoulder, dazzled her with a
grin and winked. "Hang on."*

*Revving the engine, he steered the bike into the street
and took her off on a wild adventure....*

Jillian sighed when Michael pressed her back against
the pillows, following her lead to trail kisses down her
neck. She knew exactly where he was headed and that
awareness inside her flared hotter. Stroking his glossy dark
head, she encouraged his exploration, wondered what he'd
think if he knew where her thoughts were wandering now.

She didn't think he'd mind. They'd discussed fantasies

before, and he'd wanted to know only that he was the star in them. He was. His kisses were bringing her whole body to life as he lavished them on her breasts. Desire pulsed greedily as if a powerful engine really growled between her thighs, triggering every nerve ending into such need that she couldn't help but squirm....

*Bad-boy Michael pressed back just enough to force her sundress to ride up even higher. His tight butt wedged neatly between her legs, forcing her legs even wider. His hard thighs in rough denim felt warm against her bare skin. He rocked his hips back and forth to create a steady rhythm against all her sensitive places, and she didn't know if he meant to tease her or torture her with arousal. Either way, the combination of that motion and the vibration of the engine had a powerful effect.*

Both in fantasy and reality.

Jillian stroked Michael without conscious thought. They knew each other so intimately that she didn't have to think, only touch him and respond to his touches. She only had to slice her hands over his body to feel the warmth of his skin beneath her fingertips, to lift her hips and ride his erection to make him quiver with arousal.

He indulged her breasts with a marvelous combination of gentle kisses and demanding caresses. She finally couldn't resist the need inside her. Wrapping her legs around his, she maneuvered him into position and urged him to sink inside her.

She sighed hungrily as he eased in, crowding the air from her lungs as he filled her with that glorious heat, swelling inside to touch all those places that shot a live current through her body. Raising her hips, Jillian let her body respond instinctively, met his every long languorous stroke, and strengthened the ache growing inside. She let her hands roam as freely as she allowed her imagination to run wild….

*Bad-boy Michael drove her to the parking garage at the mall. The place was packed with cars for the night-time showings at the movie theater. He had to circle through the rows to find an empty space, forcing Jillian to cling to him to keep her balance.*

*Security lights illuminated the darkness from the corners of the garage, throwing the long aisles into gloom and shadow, the sort of place where no woman would feel safe to walk alone at night.*

*She wasn't alone. Michael would never let any harm come to her. Not on his watch. When he finally maneuvered the bike to an empty space between a wall and a row of parked cars, he cut the engine and slid out of the saddle in a burst of masculine grace. He extended his hand and she slipped her own within, threaded her legs over the seat with some not-quite-unintentional glimpses of bare thighs.*

*She gained her feet then made a move to pull free, but Michael didn't let her go. He tightened his grip and crowded her against his bike. His hips bumped hers until she could feel the rock-hard erection straining inside his jeans. Tipping her face to his, she met his hungry gaze, knew in that instant they were going to kiss.*

*Swaying against him, Jillian eagerly tossed aside all her good-girl ideals for the night. She intended to enjoy a daring encounter with her fantasy man. Slipping her arms around his neck, she held her breath when he slanted his mouth across hers.*

This turned out to be a kiss unlike any she'd ever experienced. His mouth was all possession. The bold thrust of his tongue was all demand. He seemed to drink in the taste of her on each breath, to know that his boldness was making her melt inside.

Tightening her arms around him, she hung on when her knees grew liquid. With her body pressed up against his, she could feel every hard muscle of a body that would be a joy to discover. She thrilled to the wild thought.

And Michael knew, oh, he knew exactly how to press the moment to his advantage. Anchoring an arm around her waist, he braced her against him while sliding a hand under her sundress.

Jillian gasped against his mouth as he pushed aside her panties and hungrily explored her, dragging his fingers through her moist folds, pressing calloused tips inside just enough to tease and torment her.

He touched her as if he didn't need permission. By hopping onto his bike, she'd given him the right to make her respond, to take her places she'd never dared go. By her actions, she'd relinquished all control to him. Now she would answer his demands—no matter what he demanded.

She could feel the cool night air caress her bare thighs, such a sharp contrast against the heat of his hand, the fire of his touch. She couldn't see around his broad shoulders, didn't know who might chance upon them, but she knew there would be no mistaking that they were making out in a public place, not with her legs spread wide and his hand wedged between them. Not when his hips arched to ride his erection against her.

Jillian had hopped onto Michael's bike willingly. Now

*she would have to live up to his challenge or cry foul and run screaming, because he intended to push her further than she'd ever been pushed.*

*She could see it in his daring expression. She could feel it in his bold touches.*

*Splaying his hand, he forced her legs wider, riding those calloused fingers in the moisture of her desire back into places only he would dare to go. Jillian gasped and tried to close her thighs against such an intimate touch, but he only laughed...he pressed his fingers closer, not enough to penetrate, only enough to start up a throbbing that seemed to pulse through her body as an electrical current.*

*Her impulse was to resist, but almost instantly the intensity of the pleasure rendered her unable to do anything but hang on as he explored her at his leisure, as sensation surged through her until her will no longer seemed her own. Her thighs fell open wider, her body hungry for this pulsing delight that made her ride his hand to feed such greedy sensations.*

*In an instant, she was no longer worried about who might walk by, but tantalized by the thought that someone might...that they could be caught in such an erotic pose. Just the thought renewed her determination to follow where he led, to capture each sensation in case they were interrupted. She was left with this powerful ache inside, an ache only her bad boy could possibly satisfy.*

*He must have known the only thing that mattered now was his hands on her. How much she wanted him. How much he wanted her.*

*And he wanted her, no question.*

*He pushed her, dared her to protest because the possi-*

bility of her resistance and their discovery only heightened his own arousal. The question of her surrender lent weight to this moment, challenged him and empowered her.

Jillian understood. She felt caught up in the moment, challenged to be secretive, fast, bold, aware, in case someone happened by. She found herself drawn completely in by that urgency, so aroused. She, a girl who followed the rules, lived a life that while full didn't veer off too far to either the right or the left. Here she was with her legs spread wide to this man, riding his skilled fingers, wanting nothing more than for him to slip his hand down her collar and place his hand on her breast.

He must have read her thoughts.

Suddenly his hand slid up her back to her zipper. In a few fast moves, he pushed open her bodice. He didn't bother unfastening her bra, only shoved it up and out of the way, allowing her breasts to spring free in the cool night air, a gleam of pale skin in the shadows.

He let out a throaty growl, thrilling her with the knowledge of how much she affected him. Then the breath caught in her throat as he lowered his face...his mouth latched onto a sensitive tip hard enough to make her gasp. He sucked in her nipple in a slow wet pull, his tongue flicking firmly and heightening her arousal so much that had it not been for his hand between her thighs and the bike saddle behind her, she'd have melted into a puddle at his feet.

Dragging her fingers through his hair, she arched her back so he could pay sexy attention to one breast then the other while rocking her hips to the skilled pressure of his fingers.

Time ceased to exist as he coaxed her body to pulsing

*life with his intimate touches, until she forgot to breathe
because the promise of the oncoming orgasm swelled hard.
She abandoned herself to its approach, eager for the waves
of this pleasure to overtake her...until a sound penetrated
her passion-drenched haze.*

*Footsteps.*

*The steady tread of soft soles echoed over asphalt. The
hush of breathing in the thick air. The jangle of metal
against metal. Handcuffs.*

*A security guard.*

*Jillian froze, instinctively pulling away to cover
herself, but Michael wouldn't release her. He raised his
head and his smile flashed white in the darkness.
Trapping her against him, he wouldn't allow her to move,
only peered boldly down into her face as he pressed his
finger inside her.*

*Her body rebelled instinctively, a wave of gathering
muscles and hot embarrassment that made her struggle.
But he only pitted his strength against hers, no match at
all, and pursed his lips in a silent gesture to quiet her.*

*Her panic ebbed in degrees, the sight of his arousal
soothing away her hesitation. Jillian gulped a breath and,
to her amazement, the simple act of relaxing opened the
floodgates on a world of sensation she'd never imagined.
Glorious heat flowed through her, touching every nerve
ending along the way. Her body became pure feeling. Her
senses heightened to the caress of cool air on her moist
breasts, the shock of his rough hand between her thighs.*

*She sagged against him, biting back a moan that would
have alerted the guard to their presence. And Michael
knew he had her then, oh, he knew, and replied by pressing*

*that finger inside even more, intensifying the sensation, daring her to resist, to get them caught. Pleasure made reason surrender to instinct. Suddenly, she was moving, rocking her hips softly to ride this growing ache as a flashlight beam sliced through the gloom only feet from where they stood...*

*Then disappeared.*

*The guard's footsteps faded to silence as he moved away toward the next aisle of cars....*

*In one surge of motion, bad-boy Michael twisted her around, flipped her over his bike's saddle and hiked up her sundress. He shoved her panties down until they hung at her knees and exposed her bare bottom to his pleasure.*

*The shock of the air hit her hard. She tried to twist around to see what he was doing, but he placed his hand on her back to hold her still. He didn't speak, not a word of arousal or of reassurance. He couldn't. Not with the security guard moving away, still not far enough to miss any sound.*

*He knelt behind her. Digging his fingers into her bottom, he spread her cheeks wide. Then suddenly his face was there, and he dragged his tongue along all her tender places. Jillian swallowed back a moan, dissolving into a shudder that began in the pit of her stomach and radiated outward in slow spasms.*

*His tongue was suddenly everywhere, licking, probing, exciting... His stubbled cheeks abraded her aroused skin. His chin caught that tiny knot of nerve endings, pitting tender against rough. She jerked at the contact, but he didn't stop, only held her still.*

*He pressed his tongue into places that made her rock back against his face to ride him in willing abandon. But he wouldn't allow her release though he must have known she was oh, so close.*

*So close.*

*He finally stood. Covering her with his body, he ground his trapped erection against her bottom, revealing his hunger with each powerful thrust. He wrapped his arms around her and caught her breasts in his hands, kneading her greedily, pinching her nipples until she bit her lip to keep from making any noise.*

*All she could do was arch against him, blindly riding this ache inside, an ache that desperately sought satisfaction, completion. She'd never been so high, and she wanted to feel him inside her...wanted to satisfy this need...*

*But still he teased her, his leather jacket and rough jeans a sharp contrast to her exposed skin.*

*Pressing his mouth to her ear, he whispered, "Are you ready?"*

*His warm breath burst out hotly and made her shiver.*

*"Yes." Such a simple, heartfelt word.*

*He unzipped his jeans to free his erection, and Jillian held her breath, amazed at her daring, stunned by her yearning. And then he dragged that steely heat through her folds, a move so tantalizing that she didn't know anything but pleasure and the promise of the oncoming orgasm.*

*His breath shuddered in her ear, a ragged broken sound that assured her they were testing his restraint. The knowledge empowered her. She'd had no idea that her surrender could command such a tantalizing strength, but she knew in that moment it did. Abandoning herself had pushed her beyond her limits, and now Jillian would push Michael beyond his.*

*Arching her hips, she flexed her thighs to trap his erection. She mimed the motion of lovemaking, slid him along her wet desire, slow strokes that fed her hunger and made his legs shake. His hands grew still on her breasts as he got caught up in his own need. She arched her back to press her breasts into his palms, a reminder that he couldn't forget he still had a job—to push her and pleasure her.*

*In reality, she was a competent woman with a lot of control. In fantasy, she was still that woman, willing only to surrender because he proved worthy of taking the reins.*

*Chuckling against her ear, he speared his tongue inside, sent fire through her. He bit her lobe, rode her thrusts, giving as much as he took, the exchange suddenly equal, as if they were united in the goal of wringing every pleasure from the moment.*

*Then footsteps again.*

*This time they slowed to a stop so close that Jillian was wrenched from her languor.*

*Had the security guard heard them?*

*Her heart skidded to a sickening thud in her chest. The image of what she must look like bent over this motorcycle exploded in her mind. Her bra had tangled beneath her armpits. Her sundress had bunched around her waist. Her bare bottom lifted high in the air, so exposed, vulnerable.*

*They stood in stunned tableau as the flashlight beam sliced across the wall directly above their heads. Michael tensed, every muscle in his body gathering as he lowered himself against her, pressing her almost painfully into his bike saddle so the light didn't catch him.*

*She held her breath, feeling the heaviness of his body everywhere, the blaze of his erection between her legs.*

Then he eased his hand along her hip. She waited for his direction, to see if he wanted her to shift to a position that would minimize the possibility of their capture.

Michael took aim, pressed the head of his erection at her moist entrance, and pressed inside.

Jillian froze, disbelieving of his audacity. The security guard stood so close they could hear his breaths echo in the quiet. But there was nowhere for her to go, no way to resist as Michael slid in, dared so much with such a small action.

He stretched her wide and filled her, moved steadily deeper, creating an ache that renewed the arousal she'd momentarily forgotten.

It flooded back in full force now, sweeping through her on a rush of adrenaline so fierce that she shuddered violently. He paused in his efforts as the light beam sliced across the front tire of his bike, then pressed tantalizing kisses to her ear, her cheek, her temple.

He pinched her nipples but didn't let go, held her so long she thought she might cry out at the pleasure-pain jolting through her. His tenacity almost felt like a threat in the darkness, but she couldn't deny the danger of the moment, the excitement. Arching against him, she pressed close until he was in so far she could feel the delicate skin of his scrotum.

That's exactly what Michael wanted, she realized. He wanted her pleasure to override her fear of capture.

And it did. She could feel him everywhere as he anchored himself with his hands on her breasts, always kneading, teasing, tweaking. Her body heated until she knew she was on fire, the tension inside mounting until she thought she would faint without release.

*But he didn't alter his pace to bring her to completion. He only dragged his hips back, pulling himself nearly all the way out before he plunged back inside her with such power that he forced the breath from her lungs.*

*Then his control began to fray.*

*Jillian knew he was fighting his own battle for restraint because each thrust made his chest heave. His thighs began to vibrate so hard she wasn't sure how he kept standing. He pushed inside her so forcefully that each stroke made skin slap against skin until the sound echoed in the night-drenched quiet and she feared the security guard would hear them and come running. There was no possible way he could mistake the noise of two bodies joining in such hot action.*

*Still, Michael didn't relent. He buried his face in her hair. He kneaded her breasts. He reared back then drove home with thrusts that forced the air from her lungs, lifted her beyond any place she'd ever imagined she could go. And she arched wildly to meet him, to ride this mounting sensation and finally end the torture, the bliss of the moment.*

*Then it happened. Time seemed to still for a heartbeat, and their bodies froze against each other, paralyzed for an instant as their climax gathered, then they came apart in an explosion. Together.*

MICHAEL HELD Jillian, his own heart racing from the strength of his climax. She wrapped herself around him, nearly boneless as night descended into darkness beyond the French doors in their bedroom. He hadn't decided whether he felt pleased that her fantasies about him could arouse her to such fevered excitement, or intimidated that he hadn't done the job properly in reality.

He hadn't decided what the hell was going on with eavesdropping inside her head, either. But one thing was damn clear—he could hear what she was thinking.

As a kid, he'd avidly read comic books. Nothing had sounded better than possessing powers that could change an average guy into a superhero who could see through solid walls and leap over buildings in a single bound. Michael and his buds had spent more hours than he could count coming up with their own clever superhuman abilities.

They hadn't been interested in mundane stuff like the ability to fly. What good was flying when the first guy to stroll by with Kryptonite could send you to the ground?

No, Michael and his buds wanted useful stuff like super-improved brain power that would give them the ability to outthink everyone on the planet.

*That* they could have done something with. The possibilities for school alone were endless. They would have known all the correct answers on a test just by reading the questions. Much better than X-ray vision. If they knew the correct answers, then they wouldn't have actually needed to attend school.

Unfortunately, by age thirty-two, Michael had long since given up the hope of ever possessing super*anything,* which left him no damn clue to what was happening here... No, wait. He *knew* a couple of things.

After being treated to *that* lovemaking scene, Michael *knew* he'd developed the ability to hear inside Jillian's head, impossible though it seemed. A place he definitely didn't want to be when he was treated to brutal commentary about the size of his gut. Or how tight his ass *wasn't.*

He also *knew* his marriage was in a lot more trouble than he'd realized.

Just the memory of himself in leather, behaving more high-handed than he'd ever dreamed of behaving, was enough to make his body temperature spike.

And what the hell was a public parking garage all about? There was no possible way his wife would ever endure that sort of treatment from him or anybody else on this planet. He'd known Jillian nearly all her life and *knew* that without question.

But Michael wasn't stupid. He also knew enough about women's fantasies to know that a fantasy frequently had nothing to do with reality. What he didn't know was why. He tried to recall what Jillian had told him when they'd been discussing the topic after a recent Main Street Rehabilitation fund-raiser. He couldn't remember anything except that he'd wanted to try one…and had.

His body temperature spiked again. Only this time into the red zone.

His handcuffs so little resembled Jillian's encounter on a motorcycle that Michael might have laughed—if he hadn't been the star of both shows.

*That* thought made the blood throb in his ears. He was seized by such a violent restlessness he nearly jolted from the bed. On the up side, exhaustion seemed to be another side effect of fantasies because Jillian had passed out. She was so gone she didn't budge when he disentangled himself from her arms and slid from the bed.

Here was something else he *knew*—he wouldn't be sleeping tonight. Or *ever again* if he didn't figure out what the hell was going on.

Once, when his office staff had been on some health kick or another, Charlotte had told him that women looked in the mirror and saw themselves as ten pounds heavier than they were. Men, on the other hand, looked in the mirror and saw themselves as ten pounds lighter. He remembered cracking some joke about men having magic eyeballs, but he'd relegated her claim under the column of typical feminine exaggeration.

He headed into the bathroom and flipped on the light anyway.

Squinting at his reflection, he tried to add ten pounds for a glimpse at what Jillian might see when she looked at him. He did a three-sixty in front of the bi-fold mirror, suddenly realizing why men didn't spend nearly the amount of time women did in front of them.

Damn, *not* good.

He hadn't known Jillian's high-school girlfriends had been so fixated on his ass during games, but she was right about one thing—they wouldn't stop for a second look now.

Is that why she needed an elaborate fantasy to get aroused when they made love? Had she been fantasizing when he'd gone down on her, too?

Running a hand through his hair, Michael raised his gaze from the sorry sight in the mirror to find his face staring back. He looked tired and shell-shocked.

Or was that haggard and old?

He was only thirty-two for Christ's sake. Since when was thirty-two old?

Inspecting his hairline, he didn't find any gray, or bristly nose hairs, either. But he *had* put on weight.

Was he too out of shape to make love to his wife?

"Great, man, just great," he whispered to his reflection.

In addition to looking at *this* in the mirror, he got to experience performance anxiety, too.

That thought sent him fleeing into the shower in an attempt to calm down.

The pounding hot water didn't do much. His head raced with impossible thoughts—including the idea that he was really asleep right now. He'd wake up in the morning and realize that neither his superpower nor Jillian's fantasy had been anything but a dream.

He wouldn't mind waking up ten pounds lighter, either.

Michael remembered Jillian's earlier comments about her appearance, and wondered if she'd actually voiced that criticism aloud or if he'd heard her thoughts then, too. He hadn't bothered looking at her mouth so he couldn't say.

Exactly when he'd developed this impossible ability was difficult to pinpoint. Definitely since they'd arrived home from the clinic. Did this ability have something to do with sex? He couldn't say since they really hadn't done anything except have sex since arriving home. And the all-important question…did this superpower only work on his wife?

# 5

*The morning after*

JILLIAN GLANCED UP at Charlotte from the reception desk. "He's going where for lunch?"

"Swimming. At the public pool. There's an adult lap swim."

Jillian saved the spreadsheet she'd been working on and slid the keyboard tray back into its position beneath the desk. "Let me get this straight. Michael turned down your fried chicken, and instead of taking a nap while the office is closed, he's going swimming?"

"He brought all his gear in a swim bag."

And here she'd thought they were on the mend. Apparently, they'd moved into a new phase of marriage—Michael keeping secrets. "Oh."

Charlotte nodded. "That's exactly what I thought, too. Anyway, I wanted to mention it before you left for the doctor. You didn't say anything, so I wasn't sure you knew."

"I didn't. But now that I think about it, I did see him stick a bag in the trunk this morning. Never thought to ask."

And she shouldn't have had to. If the man was taking up swimming again—something he hadn't done since college—shouldn't *he* have thought to mention it?

Certainly seemed reasonable to her. "Well, I suppose this deserves a trip into the inner sanctum."

"I thought it might."

Bless Charlotte. Jillian honestly didn't know what she'd do without her. "I'll let you know."

She stood, circled the desk then headed down the long hallway that led into the back that led to Michael's office. She knocked but didn't wait for a reply before pushing the door open. She found him heading toward her, apparently on his way out, and he did indeed have a bag over his shoulder.

"You're leaving?" she asked.

"Going swimming."

"You're not going to eat?"

"Already did." He pointed to a disposable plastic container in the trash. "I brought a salad from home."

"That's a lot healthier than Charlotte's fried chicken."

"That's what I thought." He patted his stomach. "About time I exercised some self-control."

He sounded so serious the hairs on the back of her neck prickled. Jillian frowned, not sure what was unsettling her.

"Is there anything wrong, Michael?"

"No, why? You didn't have anything planned for lunch today, did you?"

"No, no. I'm going to the doctor, remember?"

"Oh, that's right. You told me this morning."

She nodded. "Swimming, Michael? I can barely remember the last time you went swimming."

"Yeah, and I'm noticing the effects on my boyish figure. Thought it was time to do something about it. If I get in better shape, maybe I won't be so tired all the time."

Well, there was certainly no disputing the reasoning. She'd said as much to him not so long ago when he'd been complaining about all the time he wasted on his midday naps. "That's it? You're not keeping anything from me?"

"Like what?"

"Oh, I don't know. But you turned down Charlotte's fried chicken. You're sure you haven't been diagnosed with some sort of terminal illness?"

With a chuckle, he caught her chin between his thumb and forefinger and tipped her face to his. "I'm fine, Jilly. No terminal illness."

He planted a kiss on her lips and headed toward the door, leaving Jillian staring after him, wondering what was really going on with her husband.

Unfortunately, she didn't get a chance to think about it because she had to deal with her own goings-on.

She felt a pang of guilt for not telling Michael *why* she was going back to the radiologist today. Her second visit in less than a month.

Then again, he hadn't asked. Nor had he asked about the outcome of her mammogram, although she'd told him she'd gone in for that, too.

He hadn't even told her he was going swimming.

Besides, one abnormal mammogram was not something to freak about, her doctor had told her when ordering this follow-up visit to the radiologist for an ultrasound.

Jillian had chosen to follow his advice.

She had a lump, but there were all sorts of lumps, most of them *not* breast cancer. Today's ultrasound would go a long way toward telling them which hers was.

And once she knew what was going on and what the doctors recommended as treatment, she'd inform Michael.

Or when he acted the tiniest bit interested.

Whichever came first.

To MICHAEL'S RELIEF his new superpower didn't work on any woman but his wife. Damn stroke of luck because all through the day as he'd been working on his patients while trying to convince himself he hadn't gone crazy, he kept remembering a chick-flick he'd seen with Jillian. Mel Gibson, who normally starred in decent movies, had been zapped by something or other that had let him hear the thoughts of every woman he saw.

Just the thought of his office and all those women, staff and patients alike...

But a day spent listening to his wife's interior monologue had also given Michael perspective. Now after Jillian had gone to bed on his first day as a husband with a superpower, he had a plan. Heading into their home office, he went straight for the only place he might find answers— the computer.

If Hollywood had made a movie about a man who could hear inside women's heads, then Michael couldn't be the first man with the ability.

Google was the place to find out.

Forty-five minutes and what felt like a thousand hits later, and Michael was forced to accept he must be the only person besides Mel Gibson ever to have this power—the only sane one anyway. There'd been a guy in Tucson who'd heard what women were thinking, along with domestic animals and urban wildlife.

Sinking back in the chair, Michael massaged his temples, trying to ease the ache growing there. It wasn't yet midnight, and he stared at the blog of the guy from Tucson, still telling himself he wasn't crazy. Not as crazy as this nut anyway.

Okay, so he could hear inside Jillian's head. Where did that leave him?

He'd never realized that his beautiful and caring wife was so chillingly matter-of-fact. A real testimony to her impulse control, Michael thought. If so much cynicism accompanied all her thoughts, then she did an amazing job of keeping it to herself. All these years and he'd had no idea she possessed such a wry view of life, or of *him*.

As much as he wanted to head to bed, close his eyes and pretend he still might wake up from this nightmare, Michael wasn't so optimistic. He'd thought about telling Jillian. She usually managed to shed valuable light on anything that came up. They shared everything…correction—he'd *thought* they'd shared everything. The memory of the leather…

No, until he had a lead on what was happening, he'd decided not to say anything. He didn't think she'd question his sanity, but wasn't willing to risk it. Yesterday, he wouldn't have had a question. But today… If his disturbingly pragmatic wife thought she acted in his best interests, he might find himself in a hospital attached to a thorazine drip.

Cradling his head in his hands, Michael massaged his temples and tried to think. If he was going to develop a superpower at this late date, why couldn't it be something useful like super-improved brain power? Maybe he could have figured out how to satisfy his wife properly. He'd been hearing her thoughts all day and hadn't figured out how to use the information…

Or had he?

He did a Google search on women's fantasies and started at the top, idly surfing page after page of information.

Women's fantasies are a normal part of sexuality. They can signal a deeper meaning that may be uncomfortable or socially unacceptable, so a woman's forbidden fantasies may only be available in her imagination. Any fantasy that increases desire for a partner is considered healthy, whether the fantasy can transition into the physical world or not.

Okay, Michael got that part. If Jillian was looking for a thrill, she would never suggest a trip to a public place—not when they knew practically every law-enforcement officer in the county. She would never risk a permanent page on the sheriff's Web site, where everyone in Natchez could type in her name, pull up her mug shot and learn she'd been busted for lewd and lascivious at Eastbrook Square Mall.

That left her to explore her fantasies in her imagination, so he searched the meanings behind women's fantasies.

Men's and women's fantasies are more alike than previously believed. Both sexes fantasize most often about being intimate with their current partner. Men's fantasies tend to be more visual and get to the sex acts more quickly. Women's tend to involve more foreplay and tactile stimulation. More importantly, women's fantasies tend to focus on the relationship dynamics between couples.

Michael would certainly agree with that assessment after being treated to a front-row seat at the leather one. Jillian had gone wild in his arms, so there was no denying the fantasy of more foreplay and tactile stimulation had enhanced the relationship dynamic between them. He wasn't going to dwell on the fact that she'd done things he'd never thought about doing with her—she'd been fantasizing about him, after all.

Michael hadn't been in top form last night anyway. Once he'd realized he could hear inside her head, his body had gone on autopilot. Now that he thought about it, the fact that he'd been able to make love to her at all had been pretty impressive. How many guys wouldn't have been able to keep it up when facing as many shocks as he had last night?

The thought made him feel better.

But he still wanted to understand what need she might be trying to fill.

Typing in Exhibitionism Fantasies, he grimaced when the screen kicked back a variety of fetish sites. He managed to dredge his way through those to some sites that provided a more psychological overview by experts on fantasies rather than a daily delivery into his e-mail box of graphic images that made his hair stand on end. Apparently there were a lot of fantasies women shared in common.

Strangers in the night: or taking a walk on the wild side
The more the merrier: or the security of being comfortable with one's body
Place me on display: or the confidence to arouse others
Sexually ravaged: or the competent woman relinquishes control

Okay, this is exactly what he was looking for—specific fantasies and the reasons behind them.

So what category had her fantasy fallen under?

Strangers in the night seemed obvious. Although Jillian fantasized about *him,* in her imagination he'd been a stranger who'd pulled up on a motorcycle and dared her to climb on.

He read the narrative on the deeper meaning of this fantasy, about how a moral and spiritual woman might find taking a walk on the wild side a liberating experience.

Michael could see the appeal. Jillian had a strong moral center. She'd been raised to believe the best about people and help whenever she was able. Her upbringing had molded her into a bit of a crusader.

Okay, when he thought about Camp Cavelier and the Main Street Rehab Project, Michael conceded she was more than *a bit.*

Definitely not the More the Merrier—thank God! But Place Me on Display and Sexually Ravaged both had possibilities.

Having the confidence to arouse others wasn't something he'd have thought Jillian would care about. Then again she had made comments about her appearance lately. She'd even mentioned her metabolism slowing down. Seemed reasonable to think she wanted to feel better about her appearance—and his.

She'd just turned thirty. Was she feeling her age? She hadn't said anything to him. In fact, her birthday had been pretty low-key because she'd been knee-deep in negotiations over the purchase of Camp Cavelier. The reasoning had possibilities, but as he hadn't been a mind reader until yesterday…

The competent woman relinquishing control fitted perfectly. Michael could definitely see the appeal—especially as she'd been buried inside one of her crusades. Was indulging in fantasy a way for her to take a mental break? If so, was there anything that he should be doing to help her?

Should he ask?

Some women can feel uncomfortable about their fantasies bridging the distance between imagination and physical.

Well, if Earnest Wernberger, Ph.D., renowned researcher of women's fantasies for the past two decades said there might be a problem, Michael would wait until he had more information before opening his mouth.

*The following week*

"DR. MICHAEL gets the first bite." Widow Serafine used her ladle to brush his hand away from the bowl. "*After* he says the blessing, of course. Can't forget to thank the Lord for good health, good food and all this wonderful company."

Michael folded his spoon into a palm, wondering if the widow intended to make the troops of campers pray before they attacked each meal. That was something he'd like to see. "Thanks, Lord, for meeting our needs today. And thanks most especially for good health, good food and wonderful company."

"Amen," everyone said in chorus.

"Now eat up, Dr. Michael, and tell me if that isn't the

best gumbo ever to warm your tongue. If you like it, I know everyone else will."

"It smells wonderful," Brandi, the newest hygienist, said.

"I thought the smell was that incense." He pointed to the small bowl of smoldering blue powder currently residing beside the sink. "A bayou luncheon ritual?"

Widow Serafine winked. "A little something extra. Thought it was a good idea to ask our Blessed Mother to keep her eyes on everyone around here. Figured it was the least I could do since y'all have been so welcoming."

"Appreciate all the help we can get around here." Michael wondered what religion this woman practiced and whether he wanted to know enough to ask.

He didn't, so he helped himself to a bite of hot soup instead. Oh, man… Closing his eyes, he enjoyed his first taste of real food in nearly a week.

"Best gumbo you ever ate, Dr. Michael?"

Wood chips would have probably tasted good right now since he hadn't eaten anything but fruits and vegetables in so long. But he didn't admit that to Widow Serafine. He just met her gaze and exhaled an appreciative sigh. "The best meal I've ever eaten. If I don't make it to the bottom of your pot—and that's a big if—I'm going to insist you let me take some home."

"I brought along plenty of plastic containers so everyone can. Sure did cook enough."

No doubt there. She'd not only served up a massive pot of gumbo, but all the side dishes right down to a home-baked key lime pie that taunted him. He'd been good for a week now. Would it kill him to cheat just one day?

But he had to admit, the combination of a lighter diet

and daily lap swims already had him feeling better. Lighter, too, even if he wouldn't venture onto a scale just yet.

But someone was going to have to eat all this food, and since everyone was indulging themselves in Widow Serafine's feast enthusiastically, he might as well join in.

Jillian caught his gaze over her bowl and smiled.

*He's so sweet. Even though he isn't happy about being involved with the camp, he has made Widow Serafine's whole day.*

Two points for him, Michael thought. But he only returned her smile. He was getting used to hearing her voice inside his head, and finding out what was happening inside *her* pretty head proved very educational.

And not all traumatizing—thankfully.

There were definite benefits to insider information. What Jillian thought and what came out of her mouth frequently weren't one and the same. He'd been taking advantage big-time. Knowing what she was thinking meant knowing all the right questions to ask.

"So how are things going at the camp?" he asked Widow Serafine. If Jillian thought he was sweet, he'd run with the opportunity to look even better.

"Things are going great, Dr. Michael." Widow Serafine replaced the lid on a crock filled with rice. "Ike's been showing Raphael around. He's already tending to the horses and making a list of what needs to be done. Figured he'd do best to prioritize before jumping into too much doing."

"Sounds like a good plan."

Widow Serafine nodded. "We're all getting to know the place. The boys did pull down the old sign at the road. Seemed like a good place to start. Raphael has been doing the building, and Philip's taken charge of carving the camp logo."

"Turns out that Philip has a knack with a wood burner, too," Jillian added. "You won't believe the new sign. It's positively gorgeous."

"The boy sure does have a gift," Widow Serafine agreed. "When the power went out after the hurricane, everyone in Bayou Doré lined up to borrow him. I swear he could start a fire with two sticks. Went through quite a spell when he was younger."

*Oh, please don't let Philip start a forest fire. I really don't need to give Michael another reason to think I can't handle this camp.*

Huh? A spoonful of gumbo curbed Michael's impulse to react. His objection to buying the camp had never been about whether or not Jillian could handle the workload—if anyone could, she was that person—but about the cost. And not just the money. Their lives were already busy enough. *Too* busy, he was now realizing as he'd been trying to carve out some time to work out.

He wasn't sure why Jillian thought otherwise, and filed that piece of inside information away for further consideration.

When he had time, of course, always in short supply.

"Marie-Louise is already planning the menu," Widow Serafine explained. "Ike showed us what the cooks have been serving up, and it's a wonder you've got campers coming at all. Canned baked beans? Thought I was going to swoon. We should serve traditional Southern food. Give everyone a taste of old home."

"There are a lot of campers, Widow Serafine. Sounds like a lot of cooking."

"Pshaw. Marie-Louise has been helping me feed the folks in Bayou Doré since she came to live there. Before that she was helping her granny feed a bunch of hungry ranch hands. And from what Mrs. Jillian tells me about the junior counselor program, we'll have plenty of assistants. Those young 'uns will all be taking turns in the kitchen, so we've got to teach them right."

"True enough." Michael knew firsthand how the program worked because he'd survived it. He'd peeled so many potatoes during his reign his hands still hurt thinking about it.

But all three years of training had been worth the effort once he'd gotten to spend the summer between his junior and senior years in the exalted position of cabin counselor. Under his rule, Company Thirteen had racked up more awards than any year since the camp opened, a record that still held today.

Michael knew because he'd checked as soon as the ink had dried on the title papers.

There'd been one perk to buying the place.

Two, actually. This old bayou granny sure could cook, and by the time he'd decided to trade his diet for the key lime pie, Michael knew the campers were going to be a lucky bunch this summer, whether or not they wound up peeling potatoes.

"You be sure to invite me for lunch on the camp's monthly visiting day," he told Widow Serafine, after they'd helped dole out the leftovers.

"You own the place, Dr. Michael. You can come for a

meal anytime." She eyed him with a grin. "I doubt you'll eat up all the profits from the looks of you."

Which was exactly what he needed to hear as he'd just fallen off the wagon with his diet. And with a smile, he maneuvered the cooler in his arms until he could shove open the back door to let Widow Serafine get through. But she stopped halfway through, shaking a bottle around the doorway.

"Just another extra," she assured him. "A few sprinkles of holy water to bless your place."

Jillian only smiled, but Michael could hear her thinking.

*Probably a good thing there isn't a church within walking distance of the camp. I can see Widow Serafine spit-polishing the campers on Sunday mornings and filing them off for services.*

Michael stood rooted to the spot in his newly blessed doorway, hands clutching the cooler. He might not understand how he'd developed the ability to hear Jillian's thoughts, but he could pinpoint when his new superpower had started—the day Widow Serafine had shown up at his office with a broken bridge.

*The following day*

JILLIAN UNDERSTOOD why Michael drove his own car to the clinic. He'd started swimming, which meant he went to the pool during lunch. He felt better, so she should do whatever she could to support him. That was her job as a wife. While he hadn't been playing from the same rulebook about Camp Cavelier, he had opened the door to finding a resolution.

Even though he hadn't once mentioned the subject in the week since they'd made up from their argument.

But Rome hadn't been built in a day and resolving this problem wouldn't happen that quickly, either. She needed to trust that Michael hadn't forgotten.

Even though he forgot everything else.

She cautioned herself to patience, but when he told her, "I've got an errand to run after work tonight, Jilly, so don't expect me home until late," and offered no other explanation, she found her patience tested big-time.

And when she overheard the new hygienist discussing Michael with their long-time hygienist, red flags started flying.

Jillian had happened across the conversation innocently enough. She'd been hidden away in the records room that doubled as her office, hashing out some unpaid claims with an insurance company. The last of the morning patients were filing out the door by the time she emerged from insurance-company hell.

Michael had said goodbye and headed out for his swim. She'd strolled toward the reception area to glance at the afternoon's schedule before deciding whether or not she had time enough to swing by the post office to mail their niece's birthday gift.

When she heard Brandi's distinctive giggle followed by Michael's name, she couldn't help slowing down. Brandi was, after all, still new to the equation, a twenty-year-old who was financing her way through night classes at the local university. This was her first job as a hygienist, and Jillian had hired the girl based upon a strong interview and employer referrals from jobs held through high school and the dental hygienist program.

In the months since starting work, Brandi had proven

professional and pleasant with a good work ethic. While she might also be overly chatty, downright giggly and just plain *young*, she'd fit in smoothly with the staff, an important part of her job description.

"It's just wrong that men can lose weight so quickly," Brandi was saying. "He's been swimming now for what—a few weeks?"

"More or less," Dianne agreed.

"Look at him. Did you have any idea he was so buff?"

Dianne laughed. "He does look good."

"For real. Do you think he wears a Speedo?"

"Brandi!"

They dissolved into laughter, leaving Jillian hastening past the open doorway with that red flag snapping in her mind.

A Speedo?

There'd been a time when Michael in any swimsuit had had girls practically drooling. He was attractive. No question. And Jillian had no trouble viewing him through a young girl's eyes. She'd been young herself once and, along with most of the cheerleading squad, she'd been head over heels with her tall, dark, handsome and thoroughly charming husband.

But the fact that barely-twenty-year-old Brandi was viewing her significantly older boss as a man hit Jillian where it hurt. Was she being over sensitive? After all, Michael's recent reversal in diet and exercise had been effecting some changes.

In an office where the staff worked so closely, it was unrealistic to think those changes should go overlooked. Still, the fact that Brandi would notice Michael in such a predatory light started Jillian thinking…

What had brought on Michael's sudden determination to work out and lose weight?

For quite some time Jillian had been after him to do exactly that because she'd been worried about his health.

She hadn't come out and nagged, of course, but she'd certainly been operating behind the scenes. Junk food had been the first to get axed from her grocery list with the belief that less temptation in the house would be healthier for them both.

But she knew this man, after all, and had for most of her life, which meant she kept coming back to the fact that Michael would never make these changes randomly. He'd had a reason for deciding now was the time to get into shape.

Should she believe that reason was as simple as he claimed?

Why was she second-guessing him?

That answer was simple, at least—because of the strife between them. She'd agreed to forgive and forget their argument if they came up with common ground about the camp. For two weeks, she'd been sitting on pins and needles waiting for them to do just that.

But life kept on, busy and distracting, and they hadn't yet gotten around to addressing the subject. Michael appeared to have forgotten—whether or not she was giving him the benefit of the doubt—and her annoyance was brewing with each passing day.

Why should she be forced to bring the subject up *again*?

If Michael really understood how important this was to her, wouldn't he follow through on what he'd said?

Shouldn't he care?

*Yes!*

But he didn't appear to care about anything but getting

back into shape, which got her thinking about the *biggest* red flag as a possible explanation—a straying husband.

Her memory flashed back to an exchange she'd happened upon not so long ago...

Brandi had been gearing up for a stint as bridesmaid in her best friend's wedding, an event that would be an unofficial high-school reunion. She'd been on a crush to look her best, shopping for new clothing and obsessing over hairstyles and makeup and jewelry to the point of delirium.

A job perk of working for a dentist was access to cosmetic niceties like laser enamel bleach and bonding.

Brandi had approached Michael for both, and Jillian's helpful husband had obliged.

*"All done." Michael stripped off his sanitary gloves and handed them to Charlotte.*

*Brandi laughed, springing out of the dental chair for a peek as Charlotte said, "Nicely done, Michael."*

*He only inclined his head graciously.*

*"Let me see." Brandi peered in the storage cabinet mirror. "My smile's so bright people won't even notice the bride. Maybe I should tell Dinah to get in here quick."*

*Charlotte snorted a laugh. "As if she could get an appointment with this man."*

*Michael moved to peer into the mirror beside Brandi and made a show of inspecting her smile. "I do great work."*

Jillian had thought nothing of the exchange at the time except to be impressed by Michael's generosity. But upon reflection, she recalled the way he'd leaned over Brandi's shoulder to peer in the cabinet mirror, so close their cheeks almost touched, for body heat to collide, to inhale the scent of Brandi's hair on a breath.

The memory zeroed in on all the hurt and discontent that had been brewing for weeks now. She'd been mulling the reasons why the camp had become such a problem, trying to find answers for questions…and now she could add a few more to her list. Such as: Was Michael's inattentiveness more than his usual oblivion to details?

And had she been missing all the signs that her husband had become unsatisfied in their marriage?

# 6

When Serafine heard the sound of a car door from outside, she pushed her chair from the supper table. She and her kin had just gathered for the meal, but she waved off Raphael. "Stay put. I'll see who it is."

Raphael nodded, understanding her decree fell under the domain of *knowing*.

Serafine *knew* their visitor wanted to see her.

Cracking the sheers on the window, she found Dr. Michael inspecting Raphael's motorbike. With a smile, Serafine made her way to the door. She always liked seeing how things unfolded. She had a job to do here in Natchez, and while she might have guessed what that job was, she wasn't sure how to accomplish it.

That was the challenge—reading the signs right. Sometimes she did. Sometimes not. Things always worked out in the end.

She pushed open the door. "What brings you our way tonight, Dr. Michael?"

He glanced away from the bike and held up a ladle. "I found this at the office. I was in the area, so I thought I'd drop by to see if you'd left it yesterday."

Her smile widened. The ladle wasn't hers, and Dr.

Michael knew it. He also knew she had something to do with the magic blooming inside him. What he didn't know was *how*. Had he figured out that part, he'd have taken matters into his own hands and likely put a fast end to the gift of *knowing* she'd shared.

"This is a great bike." Dr. Michael's gaze darted from her back to the motorbike. "Raphael's or Philip's?"

"Raphael's. He just brought it up from Bayou Doré yesterday." Which Serafine had interpreted as a *good* sign. Raphael wouldn't have brought his precious motorbike if he hadn't meant to stay a while in Natchez.

"That was a trip."

"You can say that again. Raphael had his motorbike up on a rack at first light to balance the tires. Streets in that part of town are in sorry shape after the hurricane."

"Damn shame that," Dr. Michael said. "I don't think we see half of it on the news. Speaking of, any news on how the construction's going at home?"

"Just fine from what I hear. They condemned my grandson Sam's house, which is a blessing in disguise, let me tell you. But my niece Stacey's house will be just fine with some work, which is also a blessing since she loves the old place. Once my son rips out the floors and walls and cabinets to get rid of the six inches of mold, the place will look brand new. She'll even get to pick the colors and finishes herself. After the new appliances are in, it'll be like a total remodel."

"That's the right spirit," Dr. Michael said. "I'm impressed by how so many people have been able to keep focused on the positives in the middle of so much devastation and upheaval. Jillian and I have friends who lived two blocks from the Seventeenth Street levee. Yellow-tagged. They lost both their house and their office."

"We got a lot to be thankful for. Smart folks remember it. What's a house but walls and a roof? What really matters is that the family is alive and well." Serafine chuckled. "And the pets, too. Didn't lose a one and that's saying a lot. Stacey has four cats, seven birds, a chicken and an iguana."

"That *is* saying something."

True enough, but it was what Dr. Michael *wasn't* saying that Serafine found more interesting. That he'd paid a visit to fish for information seemed obvious, but she wondered if he would just fish or if he'd jump the distance between polite chitchat to accusations of casting magic.

She couldn't wait to find out.

"Well, how rude am I, keeping you standing on the stoop. You come right in now, Dr. Michael." Swinging the door wide, she waited until he strode up the steps, plucked the ladle from his hand then used it to motion him toward the dining room. "This is a pleasure. And here I thought I'd left your break room spic and span. Must be losing my mind."

Serafine hadn't lost her mind any more than she'd lost her ladle, but she would play along. She was mighty curious to see what Dr. Michael did next.

When he hesitated, she reached outside, took him by the arm and herded him through the door. He frowned when he saw her kin sitting around the table.

"I'm interrupting your dinner."

"Of course you aren't. We haven't taken the first bite. Have you eaten yet?"

"Ah, um, I was planning to pick—"

"Then you'll join us. Marie-Louise always cooks up

enough for an army. Filling up these boys, you know. Philip already took some down to Ike, and there's still plenty. Good thing, too, because the boys can always tell when she whips up another supper with leftovers. I think she's brilliant myself, but boys will be boys." Serafine tightened her grip and kept Dr. Michael moving toward the table, pleased that Marie-Louise was already arranging another setting.

"You're sure I'm not intruding?"

"Pshaw." Serafine coaxed him to a chair beside Raphael, who extended a hand in greeting.

"Good evening, Raphael." Dr. Michael looked more at ease as he took a seat, the promise of food working another sort of magic. Nodding at Philip, he flashed a smile at Marie-Louise, who set a plate in front of him. "Thank you."

"Nothing fancy on the menu tonight," she said. "Just some pan fish and veggies. I hope you like trout, Dr. Michael."

"Whatever you're cooking smells delicious. That's really why I'm here. The ladle was only a ploy to get in the door."

Marie-Louise beamed at his praise. "Must be the corn bread."

"Or the raisin pie," Philip added with a quick glance at the counter where the pie in question cooled.

Dr. Michael followed his gaze. "I've never had the pleasure."

"Then you're in for a treat," Serafine said. "Because our Marie-Louise makes the best in the bayou. No, I take that back. The best in the South."

Philip let out a whoop of agreement, and Dr. Michael said, "Can't wait."

The man was a charmer all right. No wonder Mrs. Jillian had snapped him up. Smart woman. Serafine might not have loved her Laurent with the sort of drench-your-heart-in-moonlight-and-tears sort of love that Virginie had been so fond of, but Serafine had loved her man in her way. He'd been a good man.

Dr. Michael was a good man, too. And while she didn't know the details of what was ailing his marriage—*yet*—she knew enough about life and love to spot trouble. The disagreement she'd overheard was only a symptom of a bigger problem. Serafine needed to find out what it was.

And nothing like a little magic to shake things up.

Now she helped Marie-Louise serve up supper, and after Raphael said the grace, she decided to see if Dr. Michael was more prone to secret-spilling than his pretty wife.

"Mrs. Jillian tells me you used to visit the camp while you were growing up," she said. "She seems right fond of the place, but what I want to know is how such a busy couple makes time to manage a camp this size. The longer I'm here, the more amazed I am. A lot of traditions carrying on through the years. A lot of work. I know Mrs. Jillian is a whirlwind. And I was at your office, Dr. Michael. You're just as busy."

From the look on Dr. Michael's face, Serafine had hit the bull's-eye. No surprise there. She hadn't, after all, been shy about eavesdropping.

"Jillian thinks we can kill two birds with one stone by owning the camp."

"What birds would those be?"

"Bringing the camp into the twenty-first century and giving us a reason to get out of town on the weekends."

"Really?" Now here was one of those signs that needed reading. "Mrs. Jillian wants to work on her weekends?"

"She wants to *relax*. Believe it or not." Dr. Michael gave a chuckle that assured her he didn't. "Camp Cavelier is year-round. We practically grew up here between summers and the various celebrations and field trips. So did every other kid in Natchez. Jillian's convinced once she gets a strong staff in place, she'll have time to renovate the owner's cottage so we can have a weekend getaway."

What Dr. Michael wasn't saying, and what Serafine wasn't sure he even realized, was that his wife wanted to make time for the two of them to be together. To Serafine's mind, Mrs. Jillian had stacked the deck. Not only did this camp hold fond memories for the Landrys, but owning the place would force them to spend time here. Grand plans to be sure, but Serafine didn't need but a few weeks' acquaintance to know Mrs. Jillian was one determined lady.

"This sure would be a fun place to get away to," Raphael added, making Serafine wonder if the boy was finally going to take her advice to join forces. "We've been hearing all about the place from Ike, and there sure is a lot to do. You've got the horses, the lake and all those hiking trails. I've already surveyed the owner's cottage, and it won't take much to renovate. The place has gotten old, but structurally it's sound."

Dr. Michael set his sweet tea back on the table. "Glad to hear it. I didn't pay much attention at the walk-through before the closing. All I remember about the place was the sawdust falling on my head when I got dragged down there for a lecture the last summer I spent as a camper."

"A lecture," Philip said. "What for?"

"Relocating the newly hatched snakes into Doll House."

"Snakes?" Philip laughed and Dr. Michael nodded, his devilish grin revealing the memory as a fond one.

"Bet the girls loved that." Raphael shook his head.

"If memory serves, there was a good bit of hysteria as they evacuated the cabin, and fast, too, I'd say, given that they were all half-dressed for bed. Didn't even bother grabbing their robes."

"That's horrible." Marie-Louise set her fork down with a rattle and a grimace. "Was Doll House Mrs. Jillian's cabin?"

"It was indeed. And that was the night I decided to woo my beautiful wife."

Serafine elbowed Raphael. "We'd better be on our guard if that's the sort of pranksters who'll be coming for the summer."

Dr. Michael's baby blues twinkled. "Oh, get ready."

"You only got called down to the owner's cabin for a lecture?" Serafine asked. "From what Ike and Mrs. Jillian have said the discipline is pretty strict around here nowadays."

"It was strict back then, too. The lecture was only the start. The owners gave me three weeks of kitchen detail. I peeled so many potatoes I thought my fingers would fall off. But the real punishment was Doll House's retribution. The old owners always let the campers have a hand in the sentencing."

"Peer punishment." Serafine let out a low whistle. "Young 'uns can be downright mean. Bet that wasn't pretty."

"I was stupid enough to think I'd get off easy because they were girls. That was until they got the guys in Dreadnought to drag me out of bed in the middle of the night. Try to imagine the sort of mess a gallon of maple syrup and the dinner trash can make." Dr. Michael chuckled. "I wound up in the lake for a midnight swim butt-naked with the whole camp cheering me on. Don't know what appealed to me most—Jillian's evil mind or the way she looked in her pajamas."

Only after the laughter died away did Serafine point out that hell hath no fury like a woman—for any reason.

"True enough," Dr. Michael agreed. "As I've learned the hard way. Should have paid closer attention to Bernice and Carl's lecture instead of the sawdust."

"Must have been termite damage," Raphael said. "I noticed the signs around the foundation, but the trouble was fixed years ago from what I can tell. The drywall's not that old, and the frame is strong enough to hold up during a hurricane. Not Katrina, maybe, but close enough."

"So you've inspected the cottage and made a list of the work that needs to be done, Raphael? How much of it do you think you can do yourself?"

"A lot," Raphael said. "You and Mrs. Jillian might need to sub-contract some of the plumbing and electrical work to get the permits, but as far as the carpentry, drywall and roofing goes, Philip and I have got it covered. We can hang the light fixtures, even wallpaper or paint—whatever Mrs. Jillian wants."

"Excellent. That'll certainly make the whole process simpler. I had no idea how involved construction was until we built our house…."

Serafine liked that Dr. Michael put so much stock in Raphael's opinion. She could see the boy sit up a little straighter as they fell into a discussion about framing and rewiring. Raphael had a good head on his shoulders. He just needed a chance at working more than low-end jobs to help him focus his smarts in a proper direction. And with him to set the example, the rest of Virginie's brood would follow suit.

She had a good feeling about the whole situation. Especially when Dr. Michael bullied the conversation back around to Bayou Doré. It was a smooth effort on his part, but he got her kin chatting about the differences between the lives they'd left behind and what they saw ahead for their futures in Natchez. He fished for information about family customs and religion, specifically.

Philip seemed to be the only one oblivious to what Dr. Michael was looking for. Marie-Louise had the gift of knowing as strong as Virginie had and offered tidbits about their church, which had been damaged in the storm. She explained how the gas-station sign from across the street had shattered the beautiful stained-glass windows. Raphael said he'd been helping his great-uncle repair the steeple before leaving town.

Raphael and Marie-Louise knew they were being interrogated and wisely sidestepped any tidbits of real value, since they had no clue what Serafine had done to the man. She didn't step in to save them, either, since she was enjoying the show.

Serafine watched Dr. Michael hover on the brink of asking if the Baptistes practiced magic several times, but he couldn't seem to get the question out of his mouth. She waited until every morsel of food on the table had been eaten before deciding to put the man out of his misery.

"Well, this has been a wonderful meal for getting to know each other." She stepped into the breach when the conversation lagged, smiling when Marie-Louise seized the opportunity and bolted from the table like a jackrabbit.

"Time for pie," she said. "Hope everyone has room left."

"We'll make room for your raisin pie." Philip got up to help clear away the plates, no doubt hoping he'd earn a bigger slice.

"Now you know all about us, Dr. Michael," Serafine said. "And we know more about you and Mrs. Jillian. Leastways, what you're looking to get out of owning Camp Cavelier. You need to let us know what we can do to help."

"Just keep on doing what you're doing." He shot her a dashing grin. "And I must admit that all the good food is an unexpected perk."

"Me and my kin owe you proper, and the Baptistes always pay our debts. We're a proud bunch."

Dr. Michael waved a dismissive hand. "If you're talking about the bridge, we're square after that marvelous meal."

"Fair enough. But there aren't many jobs around that would hire on a whole family and give us a place to live. You and Mrs. Jillian have helped us out when we needed helping."

"Even trade then. Like I said, we need good people to help run this camp."

"And we will, but with my kin being so young and without a lot of references, you've still placed a lot of faith in us." She smiled and switched gears. "Sounds like you're pretty tuned in to Mrs. Jillian's thoughts. Is that true?"

Marie-Louise hid a laugh under the running water.

Raphael shot a gaze between them and scowled.

Philip dug through the silverware drawer for the pie server.

Dr. Michael's baby blues widened. His mouth popped open as if he wanted to talk, but nothing came out.

Serafine took that for a yes.

"Well," she said. "It seems to me that a man with a pretty wife who's itching for a weekend getaway should set about helping make her dream come true. Don't you think?" She met his gaze and bit back a smile. "So let me ask again, what can me and my kin do to help?"

JILLIAN AWAITED Michael's return, considering what she'd overheard at the office earlier. Had he noticed Brandi the way she'd apparently noticed him? Was he intending to stray?

From the depths of her soul, Jillian couldn't believe he would behave that way no matter what was going on between them. Aside from her dad and brother, he was the most honorable and forthright man she'd ever met.

Or was she deluding herself? Michael was a man, after all, and a very virile one, even if life currently distracted them from *that* part of their relationship. The passion had waned enough so that she'd even resorted to fantasizing….

But what about Michael's handcuffs? Didn't they prove she wasn't the only one noticing the lack? Sure, he'd claimed that she'd given him the idea after their conversation with Amelia Preston, but what else could he say? Admitting he'd needed something a little extra to get him in the mood would be tantamount to agreeing that she did look hippy in the blue dress she'd almost worn to Jenny Talbot's wedding.

Jillian didn't doubt Michael loved her. Not for an instant. Their marriage might be transitioning right now, but that was natural. After all, seven years was a milestone. The term *seven-year itch* came to mind. She knew too many couples who'd faced midlife crises and various itches in their marriages. Those crises usually started with a man buying a red pickup truck and ended with divorce papers.

While Michael might be exercising again and looking

better than ever, he hadn't mentioned anything about a new car...

Unless he was visiting dealerships tonight.

Jillian knew she wouldn't sleep and decided to do a little research on the Internet about the developmental norms of marriages. Knowledge was power, she'd always believed, and if she understood what was happening, perhaps she might come up with a better way of handling her concerns.

She only needed to buy some time—until she got a strong support staff in place. Once she had the camp under control, and could entice Michael into weekend visits away and introduce the R & R that they hadn't made time for in so long, he'd see the merit of owning the place.

She was sure of it.

A Google search yielded a variety of Web sites, and she surfed one after another until she found the site of a reputable marriage counseling agency that provided an overview of key issues challenging many couples in today's busy society and suggestions about how to keep a marriage healthy.

A loss of passion in response to busy, duty-filled lives was one of them.

The approach to analyzing a problem's cause and assessing various ways to combat the ill effects made sense to Jillian, so she bookmarked the home page. Then she read some in-depth articles about why many relationships slid down the continuum from blissfully enjoyable to barely endurable.

It was while she was reading about couples letting the weight of the world steal their leisure time that a pop-up ad stole the bulk of her computer monitor.

"Oh!" Rearing back in her chair, she blinked at the images—naked couples engaged in some shockingly graphic acts.

She closed the pop-up window.

Unfortunately, that seemingly simple act threw her into a loop of more erupting windows, image after image of bodies locked in lewd acts, body parts engaged with other body parts…skin, skin and more skin until she finally was forced to shut down the system manually to stop the show.

"What on earth is happening here?"

Scowling at the monitor, she braced for more pornography as she rebooted the system. She couldn't imagine those ads had attached themselves to the site of a reputable psychological agency. Besides, she and Michael armed all their systems with the latest in security software. Firewalls should protect them from this sort of cyber-stalking.

While her security software scanned the computer, Jillian maneuvered through the browser functions, peeking inside the system's folders to see if she could locate any file names that seemed obviously out of place. To her surprise, she found that the browser history only listed the sites she'd visited tonight.

A trip into the operating system's temporary files revealed the folder had been meticulously cleaned out, too.

*Hmm.*

Maintaining the computer fell under Jillian's domain. She regularly emptied these folders to keep things operating efficiently but hadn't touched them for several weeks. With all the running back and forth to the camp, she hadn't booted the computer, let alone performed maintenance. Michael never troubled himself. She wasn't even sure he knew these files existed, let alone were cleaned out regularly.

But if she hadn't done the deed then he must have, which left her staring at the monitor wondering why he'd developed a sudden interest in pornography.

And how much trouble her marriage was really in.

# 7

*A few days later*

"CHARLOTTE, do you mind if I interrupt you?" Michael asked, cornering his nurse inside the staff room alone.

The rest of the staff and Jillian hadn't returned yet from lunch and Michael had known he'd find Charlotte alone. Every Thursday she holed up in the staff break room with her feet up, reading the newly arrived issue of *World News Weekly,* one of the weekly magazines Jillian subscribed to to occupy patients in the reception area.

"Not at all, Michael. What's up?" Charlotte set the magazine on the table in front of her and slipped her feet back into her shoes.

"Had a question I wanted your opinion on."

"Shoot."

Michael leaned against the counter in a casual pose he didn't feel. "Did you and Larry ever talk about your fantasies?"

She blinked. "My what?"

"Your fantasies."

"Fantasies? As in *fantasy* fantasies?"

He was speaking English, wasn't he? But Charlotte's

disbelieving expression made it impossible to do anything but nod in reply.

"You're asking *me* about fantasies?"

"Well, yeah. It's sort of a delicate subject, and you're a good friend to me and Jillian. Who else would I ask?"

"Just a thought, but your wife comes to mind."

"She's exactly whom I don't want to ask. At least not until I figure out if women like to talk about this sort of stuff with their husbands."

Charlotte shook her head, clearly not getting it.

Michael tried again, trying not to sound defensive. "I read that some women feel uncomfortable talking about this stuff. Something about fantasies not being reality. I just wondered what you thought. You were married for a long time."

"How am I supposed to know whether or not Jillian would feel comfortable talking about her fantasies? I'm guessing the answer would vary from woman to woman. Listen, Michael, I'm going to give you some advice, whether you want it or not."

"Shoot."

"You married a very competent and proud woman. If you're waiting around for her to ask for your help or support then you'll be waiting forever. From what I see, Jillian asks. If you don't step up to the plate right away then you're going to get left by the wayside. She'll blow past you and take care of everything herself. Do you understand what I'm saying?"

*Huh?* "Are you referring to Jillian being comfortable talking about her fantasies?"

"Here's another bit of advice—ask your wife." Her

tone and scowl combined to make him feel like the king of the idiots.

"Guess I will." Michael beat a hasty retreat, glad he couldn't hear Charlotte's thoughts right now.

Laughter rang out from exam room five—the room where Brandi currently worked on a patient. But Jillian heard more than Brandi's girlish giggles. Her husband's deep-throated laughter floated down the hallway, too.

Jillian hung up the telephone. Ike had just called to inform her that his tractor was going to cost upwards of two thousand dollars to fix, and he needed to know what account to write the check on.

She should have been able to answer the question, but as she hadn't yet returned her accountant's phone call…

The laughter again.

Taking a deep breath, she willed her thoughts not to trail down this path again. The past few days since discovering pornographic pop-ups on the computer had been an exercise in self-discipline. One off-guard moment and her imagination conjured up images of her new-and-improved husband climbing out of a pool wearing nothing but dripping water and a Speedo while Brandi oohed and aahed from the sidelines.

The idea of Michael cheating went against everything Jillian knew about her husband. Then again, so did por-nography surfing. And turning down Charlotte's fried chicken for salad.

*Argh!* She refused, absolutely *refused* to let her over-active imagination and some weak circumstantial evidence override her common sense. She'd been married to Michael for seven years. They'd dated during high school and college. She'd known the man since Donny had brought him home when she'd been *three*.

If Michael didn't want to be married anymore, he would tell her. He would *never* sneak around behind her back with another woman. Some men might find that sort of behavior acceptable, but not Michael. He respected her too much. He respected himself.

More laughter filtered down the hall, Michael's and Brandi's. Their patient, Jillian knew, would be lying back in a dental chair, mouth open and eyes wide as she got a bird's-eye view of the hygienist flirting with the dentist.

"What on earth is Michael doing in there?" Jillian whispered to no one in particular. If anyone in the busy reception area noticed the office manager chatting with herself, they all had the grace not to stare.

But ten minutes to check a patient's mouth? This woman had been scheduled for a routine cleaning, for heaven's sake. Brandi hadn't even taken X-rays.

Jillian rooted herself to the chair, refusing, absolutely *refusing* to give in to the urge to stroll down the hall for a peek. When the phone rang, she snatched it up, grateful for the distraction.

"All right, girl," Charlotte said from the doorway after Jillian had completed the call and replaced the receiver in the cradle. "Do you want to tell me what's got you sitting on the edge of that chair looking like you're chewing nails?"

Jillian faced a decision—to 'fess up or not to 'fess up. Charlotte had become a confidant over the years, a friend whose opinion was valued. Charlotte's husband had died only a year after Michael had opened his practice, and since her kids lived on opposite coasts with their families, she'd been accepting invitations to spend holidays with Jillian and Michael's families whenever she remained in town. Nieces and nephews on both sides called her Auntie Charlotte.

But she also worked with Michael, and Jillian didn't want to share anything that might affect their working relationship, especially worries based on weak evidence.

Then again, it wasn't as if Charlotte would back off until Jillian came clean. She'd picked up the scent—not so hard to do since worry had admittedly been occupying a top slot in Jillian's thoughts the past few days. Charlotte would ask politely, maybe even ask a second time. Then, if she didn't get the answers she was looking for, she'd simply move on to interrogate Michael.

Jillian had no real choice, after all.

"Nothing's wrong," she said in a whisper, not wanting any patients in the reception area to overhear the conversation. "But I'm listening to our newest addition to the staff giggle an awful lot whenever my husband goes inside her exam room. He's been in there almost ten minutes now. Can you think of anything that interesting inside their patient's mouth?"

Charlotte narrowed her gaze and stepped inside, wedging herself strategically in the doorway so no one could approach without fair warning. "Surely you're not worried? Our newest addition is a kid."

"A very beautiful kid. And men usually go for younger women when they're having a midlife meltdown."

"I see a couple of problems with that. The first is that your husband is in his early thirties, not quite midlife."

Jillian waved a dismissive hand. "Maybe not, but turning thirty is a milestone—"

"That he reached two years ago."

"And," Jillian continued, not willing to be so easily deterred from her reasoning when her concerns had merit, "we just celebrated our seventh anniversary. Have you ever heard of the seven-year itch?"

"I have. But I've also been around longer than you, my friend. A *lot* longer. I've heard even more couples say that if they survive the first seven years of marriage, they learn how to be together. Most couples I know who've been married a long time swear they wouldn't do the first seven years again if you paid them. So where does that leave your theory?"

Jillian shrugged. "I don't know. But something's up, and Michael's not sharing it with me."

"You've talked with him?"

"Yes and no. I haven't come right out and confronted him, but I dropped hints and made myself accessible. He has had ample opportunity to discuss whatever's on his mind."

"I thought you two worked out your latest tiff."

"Tiff, right." She gave a snort of disgust. "More like Michael paid me lip service, and I bought it. Now we're supposed to go on acting as if everything is perfectly normal."

"You don't think it is." Not a question.

"We still haven't dealt with the problem, and now every flag I have is flying."

Charlotte inclined her head, willing to accept instinct even if she wasn't buying into Jillian's reasoning yet. "What's bugging you?"

"His diet, for starters. What man starts making big-time changes in his life without a reason?"

"And…"

Jillian took a deep breath, debating how forthright she wanted to be, but before she got a chance to decide, Charlotte said, "If you're worrying about putting me in an awkward position here at work, then I appreciate the concern. I also think you know better."

A laugh slipped out unbidden, and Jillian smiled, already feeling better. "I do know. You're such a good friend. I hope you know how much I appreciate you."

"I do. Now spill. I want to know what's going on between you two. You're really starting to worry me."

"Then you're in good company because I'm really starting to worry me, too. I found pornographic pop-ups on our computer."

Charlotte frowned. "All sorts of stuff sneaks around on the Web nowadays. You know that. Maybe something slipped through your firewall by accident."

"True, true, but I've got Fort Knox on all our computers. I'm not jumping to conclusions, but I can't help but wonder if it's another sign. One I shouldn't ignore."

"Like Michael's sudden interest in diet and exercise?"

Jillian nodded. "And I caught him flipping through my day planner."

"And…?"

"Why wouldn't he just ask me about my schedule?"

"Did you ask him?"

"I don't want him to think I don't trust him. We had such a nasty fight about the camp. I said…well, I said some hurtful things. I don't want to add any more fuel to the fire. I made it clear I'm unhappy with the way things have been going. I wasn't ready to end our marriage, but what if I've given him ideas?"

"Michael's pretty oblivious."

Jillian only nodded.

"For what it's worth," Charlotte said, "both people in a marriage should have their needs met. That's only reasonable. And it's reasonable to bring it up if that's not happening. Communication is the only way to keep marriage grounded."

"I know, I know."

"Really? So you told him you're going to the doctor."

"Of course."

Charlotte shook her head. "Let me rephrase that—so you've told him what's going on with the doctor?"

"He hasn't asked. And since I still don't know what's going on, I have nothing to tell. I'll let him know as soon as I get a possible diagnosis."

"Jillian, are you sure that's the best way to handle this?"

She shrugged. "No. But I'm already resentful enough about the camp. When I have to make an appointment to inform my husband about my health that he obviously cares nothing about—"

"Michael cares."

"I know, but the minute I tell him what's going on he's going to feel bad because he hasn't asked. I know the drill. Then I'll have to deal with him in addition to not knowing what's going on with me. It's just easier if I wait for a diagnosis. Then I'll know how we're going to handle treatment and involve Michael. I'll have more patience."

"You will tell him if he asks though, won't you?"

"Of course, but I don't see that happening. He's a little preoccupied lately. I'm trying to reserve opinion."

"Doesn't sound as if you're reserving opinion if you've already paired him off with Brandi."

"They've been in that room for over ten minutes." Jillian glared pointedly in the direction of the exam room. "You want to tell me what they're doing in there that's earning laughs?"

"Examining a chipped tooth, I'd guess. Brandi called him in because her patient tripped over a parking lot divider and damaged her incisor. Maybe it's a funny story. Who knows?" She frowned. "Brandi? I don't buy it. I like her well enough, but she's hardly out of her teens. Physically or emotionally."

"I happen to know she thinks Michael's attractive."

Charlotte's eyebrows disappeared into her hairline as her frown melted into surprise. "You're sure about that?"

"I overheard her talking one day and thought she was a little too interested in what my husband looks like."

"I've never heard anything that would give me the idea she thinks of Michael as anything but a friendly boss."

Charlotte's skepticism started to wear on the edges of Jillian's mood. She wouldn't be concerned if red flags weren't popping up in all areas of her life. She tried not to sound defensive when she made her case. "Brandi was speculating about what Michael might look like in a Speedo."

"Are you sure she meant it as a compliment?"

"Charlotte!"

She spread her hands in entreaty. "Come on. A *Speedo?*"

Maybe Jillian shouldn't have said anything at all. "How else could she have meant it? Michael's a good-looking man."

Something about that made Charlotte smile. "So that's all you've got—a porno pop-up, a diet, Michael's usual oblivion and the Speedo comment?"

"Something's up. I know my husband."

"That I'll buy." Folding her arms across her chest, Charlotte dropped her voice to a conspiratorial whisper. "How's your sex life?"

"Our sex life?"

"Because your husband was just asking me about women's fantasies."

"You're kidding."

"I'm not."

"What did he want to know?"

"If women liked to talk to their husbands about their fantasies."

"Did he specifically say 'talk to their husbands' or did he just want to know if women liked to talk about fantasies?"

"Husbands specifically."

"What did you tell him?"

"That he should ask you. How am I supposed to know if you like to talk about fantasies?"

Jillian might have laughed, except that Charlotte's question had gotten her to thinking about the answer. She and Michael had been so busy lately that they hadn't done much but collapse into bed when they got home at night. And now that she thought about it, she realized they hadn't had sex since…

*Uh-oh.*

"We haven't had a sex life since the night before Michael started his diet."

"Performance anxiety?"

Charlotte delivered that with such a straight face that Jillian's jaw dropped. "Charlotte! No, not performance anxiety. At least I don't think so."

"It's not as crazy as you thinking he's sweet on Brandi."

Jillian collapsed onto the desk and buried her head in her arms. She just couldn't face any more of this right now.

Husband problems. Health problems. Camp problems.

*Too many* problems.

"All right. All right," Charlotte said. "I'll keep my ears peeled and let you know if I hear anything. In the meantime, I want you to get a grip. I trust your gut feeling, but your circumstantial evidence wouldn't get a day in court."

Jillian braved a glance. "You don't think so?"

Charlotte met her gaze with a steely one of her own, her expression all earnest. "Trust me. And I'm more qualified than most to make that assessment. I'm with you two nearly as much as you're with each other. And he did ask about women talking with their husbands. Last I heard he was your husband, not Brandi's."

Just then the hygienist in question emerged from exam room five with her patient in tow. She smiled at Charlotte, who still blocked the doorway, and handed Jillian the chart. "We need to book an appointment for a bonding."

Then she bade goodbye to her patient and swept back down the hall with a bubbly laugh and a perky stride.

Charlotte shot Jillian a gaze that clearly said, "You're nuts," before she eased out of the doorway and disappeared down the hall, too.

Jillian scheduled the appointment, considering the whole time whether or not airing her concerns had made her feel better.

Yes, she decided.

At least until Michael showed up at the counter with his swim bag over his shoulder.

"I'm heading out now," he said.

"Have a nice swim."

"This is for you." He handed her an envelope before strolling back down the hall without another word.

Retrieving the letter opener, Jillian sliced open the top to find one sheet of card stock and Michael's handwriting scrawling the words:

Tomorrow night at 8:00 p.m. You and me. Alone.

She sank back in her chair. What was this?

Her earlier concerns clanged in her head like warning bells, but Jillian countered them with Charlotte's reassurances. She was overreacting.

Wasn't she?

Or was she living in denial that her marriage was in more trouble than she'd ever suspected?

*If Michael didn't want to be married anymore, he would tell her.* Her earlier thought rang out as the loudest warning of all.

Had he scheduled this appointment to tell her?

TOMORROW CAME without any of the fanfare Jillian might have expected to accompany working herself into such a frenzy. She'd had to apologize to Charlotte twice for being short, and even make amends with *Brandi,* which had stuck in her craw for more reasons than she would admit.

Now the moment of truth was at hand, and she stood inside her closet, staring at the rows of clothing for something appropriate to wear to ring in the demise of her marriage. She'd already discarded two possible outfits.

How dare Michael drag out this suspense!

He'd taken off from work today with no more than a casual goodbye. No explanation about where he was going or why he hadn't shaved. Not even a "See you at eight." He'd just strolled out the door as if he hadn't a care in the world. Perhaps he didn't, but she certainly didn't feel that way.

So how should she dress? Good enough that she'd make him regret every insensitive thing he'd ever done? Or a little disheveled so he'd think better of ending their marriage and resolve to give it another go?

Jillian pitched disheveled right out the window, mortified the thought had even crossed her mind. The very idea of being desperate enough to keep Michael through pity appalled her.

So she scanned the racks of clothing for an outfit with a pocket to keep a pen. If he asked for a divorce, she'd sign those papers so fast his head would spin.

Brave words.

But Jillian was nothing if not determined and pragmatic, so she chose a simple tunic ensemble that was flowy and feminine, dressy enough for a dinner out or casual enough for a walk in the park, since Michael hadn't seen fit to inform her what they were doing.

She applied her makeup with the precision of a Natchez Indian chief applying war paint for battle. But while determination kept her hand steady, it didn't keep her from analyzing every crack and crevice on her face. Should she have sprung the hundred-plus bucks for eye cream?

*Argh.* She squinted into the mirror. There was absolutely nothing wrong with the way she looked. She'd only just turned thirty for heaven's sake, not eighty. Michael had always liked the way she looked, and if that had changed, then the flaw was his. Maybe he was tired of looking at the same woman day in and day out. Fair enough. Looking at him didn't give her the thrill it once had, either.

At least her weight didn't yo-yo.

Jillian slipped on her shoes, a pair of stylish mules with heels low enough to walk easily in the event she was forced to whip out her pen and put on a good show, yet easy to remove in case she gave in to the urge to beat her husband with them. And just as she emerged from the closet, she heard noise…a loud noise that seemed to be coming from outside.

The low roar of a motorcycle.

No one on their block owned a motorcycle that she knew of, but the sound didn't pass—it grew louder. Making her way into the living room, she pulled aside the sheers on the side light beside the front door and peered out into the street.

Spring meant that dusk was only now making an appearance, slicing across the fading sky in streaks of vivid pastel. She usually loved this time of year. The heat of summer hadn't settled in yet, but the chill of winter was gone. Perfect. The kind of nights where she would grab her laptop and work outside on the deck beside the pool while the cicadas chirped and starlight twinkled overhead.

One glimpse into the street revealed a man in black leather driving what had to be the biggest chopper she'd ever seen in her life. Jillian wouldn't have been surprised to find Michael pulling up in a red truck with divorce papers in hand, but when this big, bad biker made his way into *her* driveway, she could feel her eyes practically bulging out of her head.

Of course Michael was no where to be found when she needed him to answer the door and find out what this biker might want.

She could ignore the door, but wasn't inclined to let a man's appearance frighten her off. Who knew, he could be one of their policeman buddies representing the biker organization that hosted the annual fund-raiser, Ride for Kids.

And there was something familiar about him....

When he heeled down the kickstand and got off the bike, *everything* about his strong, fluid movements seemed familiar.

She blinked then did a double take.

*Michael?*

If she still wasn't convinced, Jillian watched as he removed the helmet and hung it on the back rail.

*"Oh my God!"* she heard herself say. "Not a red truck but a chopper. The man really is having a midlife meltdown."

She stood there, unable to do anything more than stare as he strode up their walkway, looking as casual and content as if life hadn't just turned end over end.

She was still staring when he knocked on the door.

Knocked?

Jillian forced herself to open the door. She did not step aside or let him enter. She left him standing on their porch, uncertain how to greet him and dumbstruck by how a costume change had altered everything she knew about this man.

He might be her husband, but he wasn't *Michael.*

The man standing on her front porch sported a two-day stubble that shadowed his cheeks, hardened the lines of his jaw and deepened the blue of his eyes. The leather jacket made his broad shoulders even broader. The tight pants showed off his trim hips and newly-toned butt to perfection. The butt of her high-school memories.

This man could have been the bad-boy Michael of her fantasies, which made the reality of their troubled marriage drive a knife into her heart.

"Are you ready?" He sounded as laid-back as if they were leaving for work the way they did every morning. "You should probably grab a jacket."

"Michael, what's going on?"

She sounded calm for a woman staring at her husband masquerading as a stranger.

He flashed a grin that managed to be even more dashing against his stubbled cheeks.

Jillian wasn't sure what she expected, but it wasn't for Michael to take her hand.

He brushed his mouth across her knuckles in a poignant move from their past. Once upon a time, when they'd been young and in love, Michael would always gallantly kiss her hand and she would sigh the most heartfelt of sighs.

Now she could only think to ask, "Are you having an affair?"

Still holding her hand, he peered up at her with bedroom eyes, a look that used to melt her knees underneath her. He shook his head slowly, still not letting her go. "Not yet, but I'm going to be."

The breath solidified in her throat, just seemed to harden into a knot that she thought would choke her. Or make her pass out. Clutching at the door with her free hand, she needed some anchor to hang on to as her head spun dizzily.

But she refused, absolutely *refused* to let Michael see how his news impacted her. If he could casually deliver that statement with no thought for her feelings, then she would accept the news just as casually.

"Oh." She managed a calm she was far from feeling. "Well then, do you mind if I ask with whom?"

She braced herself to hear the name of a saucy little hygienist who giggled too much, when with all her heart she wanted to hear words of reassurance that their marriage wasn't in desperate trouble.

Michael only smiled a thoughtful smile that looked so different now. His gaze went even softer, a sure sign he was head over heels for whoever his girly-girl was.

She braced herself when he tightened his grip on her hand and said, "You."

# 8

___

FOR A MOMENT, Jillian looked so utterly shocked that Michael thought he might have to catch her—not exactly the reaction he'd been going for. But she hadn't laughed in his face and he supposed that was something.

Not that he would have blamed her.

This whole fantasy idea had seemed brilliant while sitting at Widow Serafine's table—the perfect solution to reawaken the passion in his marriage. Of course, at the time he'd been groggy from rich food and influenced by Widow Serafine.

That crazy old bayou granny had been pushing so hard for him to make Jillian's dreams come true that he knew without a doubt she was responsible for his superpower.

Not that he could rationally explain it, nor would she confess.

But all Widow Serafine's references about reading Jillian's mind were the only confirmation he needed. The widow knew more about his marriage than he did. Since he didn't think Jillian would share personal information with a new employee, he'd guessed that Widow Serafine must read minds, too. That would certainly explain how she'd managed to share the skill with him. And at this stage of the game, about the last thing he wanted to do was tick off this bayou granny. Which meant following her not-so-veiled suggestions.

As far as Widow Serafine was concerned, Michael would be a fool not to make the most of opportunity when it knocked. Since he owned the camp, he should use it, especially since his wife had grand plans for the place.

And that's exactly what he intended to do.

Lifting Jillian's hand back to his lips, Michael brushed his mouth across her knuckles and raised his gaze to hers. "I want to have an affair with you, Jilly my love."

There, he'd said it. The words didn't sound nearly as stupid as he'd thought they would.

Especially when Jillian melted around the edges, that look she always got when she was underneath him. A look that made him feel as if he performed magic.

"An affair, Michael? But we're married." She gave a soft chuckle. "You have me at home, at work. You can't get away from me no matter how hard you try."

"I'm a lucky man." He brushed his mouth across her knuckles again. "But you're talking about reality. I'm talking about fantasy. We're going to leave the real world behind tonight."

Her gaze darted over him again, taking in the black leather in a glance, and the lines deepened around her beautiful mouth.

"An affair, Jilly. You don't have to do a thing but let me sweep you off your feet."

*Oh, I hope he hasn't lost his mind. So what do I do now—get on that chopper? Or should I call Jimmy Dooley and ask him to send a cruiser?*

Michael didn't have any trouble visualizing the burly

sheriff who'd been a friend since the seventh grade. He hurried to explain. "I just want to relax and have fun. We used to squeeze in our life around our relationship. Nowadays, we're squeezing our relationship into our life. Or trying to. Between work and the camp, we don't have enough time for each other. I miss my wife."

Jillian's frown began to fade.

*Oh, how do I know he's all right? I mean, really all right? What if he's having a nervous breakdown? What if I pushed him over the edge with all the stress about the camp?*

Michael thumbed her hand, enjoying the feel of her silky skin, a simple touch, and a potent one. Surely she felt it, too. That chemistry was still between them, still alive after all these years.

"For a long time, we've been talking about making more time for us," he explained. "I'm tired of talking. I've been getting back into shape, so I won't be so tired all the time. I want to look good for you."

His admission hung in the air for a suspended instant, and he waited, feeling raw and exposed, an unfamiliar feeling that he wasn't crazy about.

"I think you're the most handsome man in the world. I always have." The words tumbled out in a breathless rush that did a lot to assuage his pride.

"Then let's have an affair."

He caught her gaze and held it, willing her to see that he felt the same about her.

She looked so beautiful in that moment with her reddish-gold hair tumbling around her shoulders, her smooth skin glowing with a faint hint of a blush, her expression all indecision and wary excitement.

He recognized the moment when she decided. Her chest rose and fell on a sharp breath. She finally met his gaze with a promise in her eyes.

"All right, Michael. Shall I change or am I dressed okay for whatever you have planned?"

"You're perfect. Just grab a jacket."

With a quick nod that sent waves tumbling around her face, she spun on her heel and disappeared down the hall toward their bedroom, everything about her tentative and excited.

He watched as she reappeared in the hall, shrugging on a jacket, still blushing and breathless. He armed the security system. She locked the door behind them. He helped secure her helmet then pulled on his own.

"Climb on behind me and wrap your arms around my waist," he told her, and Jillian slid into the saddle then nestled up close, her cheek pressed to his back, her parted thighs tucked neatly around his.

"You ready?" he asked.

She tightened her arms around him, and Michael wheeled the bike out of the drive, pulled back on the throttle and took off for their night of fantasy.

JILLIAN snuggled against Michael's back as the bike roared down the street. With her arms tight around his waist, she hung on, her cheek against soft leather, imagining rather than smelling the familiar scent of his skin.

She couldn't help but smile. The only thing that felt important right now was knowing her marriage wasn't in pieces.

Michael hadn't forgotten about his promise to deal with the camp. He hadn't been ignoring the problem, but coming up with a way to handle it. While there were obstacles ahead they'd still need to overcome, he loved her enough to make lifestyle changes and begin addressing the problems.

To surprise her with a fantasy night because he missed her.

Her worries about Brandi appeared to be groundless, just as Charlotte had said. Had he been surfing the Web for information about fantasies? Is that how the porno pop-up had gotten onto their hard drive?

The explanation seemed likely. But Jillian wouldn't ask. Not tonight. Michael obviously thought fantasy was the place to begin addressing their issues.

And it was a start.

She'd place her concerns and resentments aside for the night and follow where he led.

The wind snatched hair from beneath the edges of the helmet as she caught sight of Mrs. Vineson peering through a sidelight from her house at the corner of the cul-de-sac. Was the stately matron, who currently served as president of the subdivision homeowners' association, trying to make out who'd had the nerve to ride a motorcycle through their neighborhood? With any luck she wouldn't recognize Dr. and Mrs. Landry as the culprits responsible for making such a racket on this tranquil spring evening.

But Jillian decided she didn't really care what Mrs. Vineson thought. Michael had obviously gone through a great deal of effort to arrange tonight. Not to mention the effort of his daily swims and turning down all the food he loved.

*I wanted to look good for you.*

Snuggling closer, she was amazed at how quickly that giddy awareness rushed her, a recognizable feeling from years of giddiness about this man, affection so real it had substance.

She'd missed Michael, too, and couldn't help but wonder what had made him decide to take her on a motorcycle ride. He looked so much like her fantasy bad boy that if she hadn't known better, she might have thought he could read her mind. The very idea made her body temperature rise with a heat that didn't cool until he drove over the bridge.

Her sense of anticipation grew as the wind stung her cheeks. The state line between Mississippi and Louisiana ran smack in the middle of the river, and it looked as though whatever fantasy he'd planned for tonight would take place in a different state. A sense of freedom claimed her, as if crossing the state line magically placed their daily life and everyday routine behind them.

They were on an adventure that took them to the Astaire, an historic theater that featured an odd mix of vintage film runs and blockbuster sneak previews. During their school years, the Astaire Theater had hosted acting companies that toured the country with a variety of educational performances. Fairy tales. Classics. Myths. Legends. Fables. All had come to life on the grand old stage.

While Jillian wasn't sure if the tradition still continued, she did know the theater had been upgraded with modern conveniences to keep the interest of a movie-going crowd used to surround-sound and stadium seating.

Michael turned over the motorcycle to a valet and

helped Jillian remove her helmet. Then, with a smile that made her pulse race, he tucked her arm through his and pulled her close enough so she could feel the hard lines of his body all warm and familiar, feel the promise of being together in a way she hadn't in so long.

"Ready?" he asked.

"We're seeing a movie?"

"Think of tonight as a first date of sorts. If memory serves, we missed an opportunity at this theater once."

It took a minute to pinpoint what he was talking about. "Michael, are you talking about that high-school field trip when we first started dating?"

"You wrote me a letter about what might have happened in this theater if I'd been with you. Do you remember?"

She remembered the note, but was surprised that he did. "I resented missing our lunch period together for a field trip for a stupid play."

"So you wrote."

"I would much rather have been flirting with you in the lunch room."

So much rather, in fact, that she'd spent the entire bus trip—when she could have been chatting with her girl-friends—writing that impassioned note about all the things she could have been doing with him. Sexy things. Or so they'd seemed at the time.

"You do realize that we've done everything I wrote in that letter and then some."

Catching her chin between a thumb and forefinger, he tipped her face to his. Was it a trick of the setting sun or the leather that made Michael look like a sexy stranger?

"We've never done it inside a theater."

Jillian's heart began a dull thud in her chest. Surely he wasn't suggesting—

"You ready?" He released her and swept an arm toward the ticket booth.

She stared up at him, poised on the edge of a place she hadn't been for years.

Excitement.

It was a feeling she remembered from the past, a feeling she remembered from every sexy first they'd ever shared…the first time they'd kissed…the first time he'd touched her…the first time they'd gotten naked together…the first time they'd made love.

She wasn't sure what Michael expected tonight and squelched the naggy voice inside reminding her that she and Michael were no longer kids who could tempt fate and survive with their reputations intact. The very thought of having to call Jimmy Dooley to pull strings and spring them from jail…

His smile dared her, sparked a rebellion inside. And Jillian knew she wouldn't respect herself if she didn't rise to his challenge, and counter with a few of her own.

"I'm ready." She looped her arm through his.

His gaze assured her that that response was exactly what he'd hoped for. And as he fished out a credit card from his wallet to pay for tickets, Jillian combed her memory for what she'd written in that long-ago letter.

Making out. Melodramatic vows of eternal devotion. She'd been so young, only a sophomore in high school, and it was long before they'd first made love. The passion and innocence of that time made her smile as he collected their tickets and led her inside.

"Popcorn?" Michael asked.

"No, thanks." Junk food was about the last thing her stomach needed after the emotionally unsettling past few days, and she didn't want to tempt Michael.

He was looking *so* good.

They settled on a diet drink to share, made their purchase and headed inside the theater.

This weekend wrapped up Vintage Movie Month, and from the quiet of the place, Jillian guessed that anyone who'd wanted to see a vintage movie had already seen one. Save for a handful of couples and a group of teens with primary-colored hair and facial piercings that glinted in the low light, the theater was dismally empty.

Michael led her all the way up to the last row into seats directly beneath the projector room. "You okay sitting up here?"

"Depends on how well you want me to see the screen."

"I'm only interested in how well you can see me."

His voice was all throaty innuendo, all promises in the dark. A shiver coursed through her.

"Up here will be fine."

The shadows sliced across his features until he didn't look like her husband at all. His grip was firm as he led her to a seat. He removed his jacket and settled in beside her, and she wasn't surprised when he flipped up the armrest and pulled her close. "Come here."

Jillian nestled against him, amazed by how a simple costume had changed everything about this man. Even the feel of his body was different tonight, a combination of his newly honed physique and the suggestion of sexy games in the shadows.

Needing to hear something familiar to anchor her to the moment, she asked, "I didn't notice the feature. What's playing?"

"A vintage chick flick."

Tipping her head back, she gazed into his face. "But it's not my turn. You're supposed to see one of your Neanderthal action adventures next."

"Forget the rules tonight. We don't have to make compromises. We're both going to enjoy ourselves."

And his tone promised that the enjoyment didn't have a thing to do with the movie.

"No rules and no compromises, hmm?" She liked the sound of that. "Is this a freebie, or are you planning to make me pay?"

"Nice try, Jilly, but no freebies. Plan to pay big."

His low laughter filtered through the quiet, filtered through *her*. She could practically feel the sound winding through her, arousing every nerve along the way. His deepthroated admission spiked the awareness of the moment, a physical sensation that awoke places inside she hadn't even realized had been asleep.

What was it about this man that touched her so deeply?

Jillian had come up with lots of answers through the years, some involving his various qualities, others about the way he looked or made her respond to him.

Tonight Michael's appeal was all about a motorcycle ride across the river, about a diet and daily swims to make himself more attractive.

Tonight was all about his efforts to create a fantasy.

He missed her.

She missed him, too.

And as the trailers ended and the lights dimmed in preparation for the feature to begin, Jillian found her tension ebbing away, tension that had become such a natural part of her lately that she hadn't even realized she felt tense.

The pressure of the thousand things that constantly warred for attention in her mind quieted until she could focus only on the characters on the screen. On the feel of Michael's arms around her, and the way she fit perfectly into the curve of his body.

A hush had fallen over the theater and the only sounds were the voices on screen—the dialogue of real voices as opposed to the roar of sound effects—and the whisper of his breathing.

When Michael ran his hands down the length of her arms, strong, soothing strokes, she relaxed against him, willing to follow where he led.

An affair.

Jillian smiled into the darkness, wondering just how far he would go to create a fantasy night—how far she would let him go.

He obviously had a plan, and the languid warmth stealing through her chased away reality. The antics on screen suddenly couldn't compete with his familiar male scent layered with the hint of leather.

Especially when Michael maneuvered them around until she could sink back against him for better access, feel his swelling crotch against her bottom. She let her eyes drift shut to narrow her focus to the feel of his touch, the simple strokes that somehow felt as intimate, purposeful caresses.

Michael was clearly in no rush. Easing his hands down her arms then back again, he lulled her into a daze that made her feel better than she did during her massages at the Under-the-Hill spa she visited with her old cheerleading buddies on their girls' weekends out.

There was an intimacy that only a lover could bring to his touch, a familiarity that somehow hinted at all the pleasures they'd shared together, a reminder of how he could so easily arouse her, tempt her.

His caresses carried a promise of greater pleasures to come. Just the firm strokes of his palms down her arms mounted her awareness…drew her attention to the silky fabric of her clothing that shielded bare skin.

Somehow he knew that she wanted to feel skin against skin because he extended his reach to her hands, curling warm fingers over hers, pressing the tips between hers in such a simple but erotic move.

Jillian had always loved his hands, long-fingered and strong. Whether he reined in his strength to do the delicate work of dentistry or aroused her with skilled touches, Michael used his hands to incredible effect. And she'd always loved the way his hands looked when he touched her.

Opening her eyes, she fixed her gaze on the sight of his hands slowly caressing hers. His skin tanned. Hers pale. A sight that managed to make her feel so in tune with him.

The movie droned on, a blur of voices and laughter. Someone in the audience whispered to a companion. Another shifted around restlessly until the chair squeaked out a reminder that Jillian and Michael weren't alone in the monochromatic darkness.

To her surprise, the reminder only spiked her daring. There was something exciting about Michael's touch, about how he could make her forget everything but the feel of his hands on her.

This, too, was a feeling she recalled from the distant past. Once she'd been a young girl obsessed with him. Her days had been no more than minutes strung together spent imagining the ways he might touch her, the ways she might touch him back.

A memory flooded her mind, striking and cherished...
*They were tearing down the stairs between classes, unable to walk arm in arm or hold hands because they were juggling too many books. Jillian wanted to hold Michael's hand, resented that she was denied a perfect opportunity to touch him because of logistics. Who needed AP chem, anyway?*

*Michael must have been thinking similar thoughts because he gazed down at her with an expression that thrilled her straight down to her toes, a hunger in his eyes that assured her if he didn't touch her soon he'd never make it through the rest of the day.*

*Jillian smiled an invitation, and that was all the invitation Michael needed. He nudged her out of the crush of students. He dropped his books onto the floor with a noisy clatter. He crowded her against the wall until she had no choice but to drop hers, too.*

*Laughing at the sheer wildness of the moment, she wound her arms around his neck.... His lips came down on hers, a greedy exploration. The moment was fleeting and he intended to savor the contact before she was stolen away.*

*Jillian dissolved in his arms, swayed against him, wanted to feel every hard inch of him to satisfy the longing she felt burning inside. And Michael knew...oh, he knew because he didn't care that they were drawing attention.*

*He didn't care that a teacher could walk by and bust them at any second.*

*He only cared about touching her.*

*Maneuvering a hand between them, he molded his fingers around her breast, felt the warm weight of her in his palm. A tiny moan slipped from her lips, burst against his, and Jillian could only melt against him when he squeezed lightly, so undone by his touch that she forgot they were in public....*

Suddenly, Michael dragged his fingers down the curve of her throat. She couldn't remember how his hand had gotten there, but she wasn't surprised his touch mirrored her thoughts.

Michael had always known how to satisfy her, even before she'd known herself. Splaying his palm on her chest, he dipped his fingertips beneath her neckline, a suggestive touch that hinted of all the places he might go if Jillian dared.

Did she dare?

A movie-goer chose that moment to stand and maneuver through the seating toward the aisle. Another concession run or a restroom break. Jillian watched him descend the stairs and disappear, attention drawn to the dozen-odd folks scattered around the theater, any of whom could simply turn their heads and catch her and Michael in the act.

Was Michael thinking similar thoughts? Did he find the thrill of the moment as enticing? As tempting? As forbidden?

A vision of climbing into a police cruiser popped into her head, along with having to make explanations about why a respectable doctor and his wife had been caught exposing themselves in public.

Michael clearly wasn't daunted by similar worries. His

crotch swelled against her backside, a precursor to an erection. He curled his hands over her breasts, not quite touching, but more of a tantalizing promise to convince her to take a chance and follow where he led.

Her breasts grew tight and heavy. And as if he could sense her response, Michael's hands lingered, testing, waiting to see if she'd pull away or encourage him to further exploration.

Jillian debated. She felt so warm and languid, hovering on the edge of arousal, tantalized by the bold promise in his touch, yet still cautious.

Did she dare?

The promise of pleasure was fast melting away her propriety, a promise that heightened her daring.

Fantasy or reality?

She knew which Michael wanted. He'd set out to create a fantasy tonight, so much more than handcuffs. He wanted to explore the past and break through boundaries and the familiar routine of their present. The problems.

She only had to let him.

No rules. No compromises.

Arching her back, an oh, so slight move that changed the dynamics completely, Jillian pressed her breasts into his palms in sexy invitation.

With a throaty chuckle, Michael dragged his hands over her, a firm touch that made her breath hitch and her body tingle. He thumbed her through the filmy tunic, a steady motion that gathered her nipples into tight peaks that strained against soft silk, creating a friction she could feel everywhere.

Letting her eyes drift closed again, she rebelliously blocked out anything but the feel of his hands on her.

No questions. No worries. No fear.

She gave herself over to the moment as he touched and stroked and kneaded. Arousal awakened. Pleasure mounted until she found it hard to sit still. Desire pooled between her thighs, a warm and achy sensation, an insistent ache that made her crotch grow warm and moist in her panties, made her grateful her clothing kept the situation under control.

So she thought.

Suddenly Michael popped the buttons on her tunic, allowing the fabric to gape open and expose her bra. She inhaled sharply and swallowed back an instinctive protest. Surely Michael wouldn't dare…

He popped the fastener of her bra.

Her breasts spilled out in a tumble of pale skin. Her nipples puckered against the sudden coolness, a greedy gathering that contrasted the growing warmth between her legs.

Jillian shivered.

He caught her nipples between his thumbs and forefingers and gave a good squeeze, proving that he did indeed dare.

The gasp that escaped from between her lips echoed in the muted quiet of the theater and earned a low chuckle from her fantasy man, who bent his head low until they were practically cheek to cheek.

"Shh," he whispered, a sound that gusted warmly against her ear, filtered lazily through her. "You don't want to get us caught, do you?"

He pulled her nipples again, hard enough to jolt more heat through her.

She bit her lip to hold back another gasp.

Exactly how was she supposed to *shh* when he started

plucking her nipples and fondling her breasts until she was practically melting?

Her only consolation was that she wasn't the only one so affected. Michael rocked against her, nudged his crotch against her backside to ride his own ache, assuring her he was with her in enjoying the challenge of the fantasy, the dare.

She barely recognized this Michael, this man who remembered love notes from the past and had shown up in leather. But if he wanted to push the limits between them then she would follow where he led.

She wouldn't dwell on how she would look if a theater employee showed up with a flashlight, or how she would feel about facing charges for indecent exposure.

Jillian would let reality fade beneath the delicious feeling of the forbidden, and savor the fantasy as her own.

So when Michael plucked and tugged and teased until she could no longer sit still, she rocked against him, savored the feel of his growing erection against her backside, the knowledge that she was tempting him as much as he tempted her.

And when he popped the remaining buttons on her tunic, one by one, he dared her to protest....

With her eyes pressed tightly shut, Jillian just held her breath, determined not to give in to worry or fear. She reminded herself that Michael had his eyes wide open. He wouldn't let anything happen to her.

This moment was all about pleasure.

But the breath skittered in her throat when he parted the tunic and slid his hand down her bare stomach....

Beneath the waistband of her pants.

She'd dressed in this tunic ensemble for the sheer anonymity of an outfit that would make her feel dressed for the uncertainties of the night ahead. It had proved to be a good choice because the elastic waistband gave Michael easy access.

And access he did.

Sliding his hand over her abdomen and spearing his warm fingers right between her thighs.

Jillian almost came up out of the seat.

"Shh. There's a couple a few rows ahead that keeps turning around to check us out. I think they can hear you breathing. You sound excited."

She *was* excited.

Jillian glanced around the audience but couldn't see anyone turned toward them. It didn't matter anyway because Michael curled his fingers over her sex, honing in on that tiny bundle of nerves that vanquished worry beneath a wave of sensation so intense she sighed aloud.

He laughed against her ear, his warm breath making her shiver.

Jillian let her eyes drift shut again, uncaring about anything except the feel of his hands on her.

Ten points for familiarity.

This man knew her body. He knew just where to touch her for maximum effect. Sure, they might sacrifice some of that wild passion of youth, but she'd take the trade-off any day.

And, besides, the man touching her right now wasn't the same Michael she lived with day in and day out.

*That* Michael had seemed quite content living in the reality of their busy days. He'd never worn black leather, or ridden a big black chopper, or been so bold as to pleasure her in a public theater.

*This* Michael seemed turned on by the possibility of exposure and the threat of potential consequences. He ground his erection against her in a rhythm that proved he was.

And when he eased a finger between her thighs, Michael convinced her once and for all that her charming and a bit-too-complacent husband had truly turned over a new leaf. He tightened his grip, still toying with a tender nipple, as he dragged his fingers through the wet folds of her desire.

Jillian's breath came in tiny gasps as her sex spasmed, suddenly greedy for his attention. He eased his fingertips inside, just enough to tempt and tease, to make her rock her hips to indulge such a lovely sensation.

Slipping her hand over his, she added pressure, just enough to press his finger in a little more. That felt *so* nice....

Massaging her sex knowingly, Michael lowered his head until his face fit into her the curve of her neck and he could rain sexy kisses along her throat. He plucked at her nipple, earning another shiver, and Jillian melted into a dreamy haze of sensation, a place where fantasy and pleasure collided.

She didn't know another thing except the mounting of the oncoming orgasm until a sound ripped through the quiet and Michael stiffened against her as if startled.

She opened her eyes to find the film frozen on screen. When it dissolved into snow, someone groaned loudly. Someone else let a curse fly toward the projection room. A couple stood and informed everyone they'd report the trouble to management, which earned mutters of thanks. The remaining moviegoers erupted into chatter, taking advantage of the unexpected intermission.

Jillian forced herself up from the warmth of Michael's

embrace, intent upon righting her clothing in case the house lights came on, but Michael wouldn't let her go.

Instead, he slid his finger inside her.

"Michael," Jillian gasped out on a breath, finding her strength pitted against his when he tightened his grip more.

"Shh, or someone will hear you."

No doubt. Only the sounds of chatter filled the darkness. The other moviegoers seemed so near, a part of this new little world of boldness and daring. Another couple stood and headed out of the theater, maybe frustrated with the interruption, maybe to use the break for a concession run.

Jillian sat on the brink of a decision. She knew Michael would let her go if she insisted. She also knew that he'd made his stand—he wanted to pleasure her. She only had to decide.

Fantasy or reality?

Tipping her head back, she gazed into his face, recognized the challenge in his expression, the hungrily bold look in his eyes. He dared her to continue, emphasized his point by kneading his palm against that sensitive place until she squirmed.

Jillian tried not to dwell on what she must look like with her breasts exposed and Michael's hand buried between her thighs. She just gave over to the mounting pleasure and rode his hand toward one of those oh, so sweet orgasms that always left her weak and gasping.

# 9

MICHAEL LEFT THE chopper idling in the driveway as he helped Jillian off. The warm spring sunset had cooled into a brisk night. Darkness had fallen so completely that the streetlamps barely threw enough light to see the straps of her helmet. But he couldn't miss her nipples straining against her silk blouse.

"You're cold." He pulled her jacket closed. "You need to get inside and warm up."

She glanced at him, surprised. "Aren't you coming?"

"Inviting me inside after one date?"

She nodded.

*Of course I am, you silly man. I want another of those yummy orgasms…or two. And I'll make it well worth your while, I promise.*

No damn doubt.

Especially when she did her best temptress impression. Swaying in a full-bodied move, she pressed against him, and the feel of her curves, warm and yielding, kicked his seriously tested libido into overdrive.

She gazed into his face, looking all dreamy and sated. "Are you saying you don't want to make love?"

He didn't bother with a denial. Not when proof of where

he stood on the issue currently rose between them and grew even harder with each passing second.

Michael wanted nothing more than to curl up in their warm bed and finish what he'd started. His temptress was an accommodating wife on a normal day. No doubt she'd make magic happen tonight.

But the whole point of this fantasy date was to reignite the passion in their marriage. He'd done his research and knew one night wasn't going to do the trick. Not by a long shot. He wanted lasting results. Widow Serafine had given him the home-team advantage, and he intended to use it.

Even if it killed him.

Michael thought it might. Jillian snuggled against him with a vengeance, still turned on and seemingly determined to take him with her. She rocked her hips back and forth in a sultry motion and was blowing his careful restraint straight to hell.

"Think of this as our first date, Jilly. We're going to get to know each other better."

Rearing back, she gazed up at him. "Really?"

*Get to know each other better? Has the man lost his mind? I know exactly what foods give him gas. What more could I possibly need to know?*

Ouch. And just how had he missed this streak of brutal pragmatism after seven years of marriage?

Michael didn't know and didn't ask, but there were definite moments when he waxed poetic about the days before he had possessed his superpower. This was one of them. Whoever said "ignorance is bliss" had hit the nail on the head.

Brushing errant waves from Jillian's neck, he

skimmed his fingers over the pulse that beat low in her throat, a rapid-fire rhythm that did a lot to restore his confidence. Gassy foods aside, he still knew how to arouse his wife.

"I'm not talking about the *real* stuff," he explained. "I'm talking about fantasy. I want to learn about what's going on inside your head, about what turns you on. I want your help bringing the romance back into our lives. I want to explore the deepest, darkest secrets about what turns you on."

"*My* deepest, darkest secrets? What about yours?"

"Mine, too."

"You're not planning to show up at the office in leather, are you?"

He eyed her narrowly. "And here I thought you were the straight man in this relationship? No, I'm not planning to show up at the office in leather."

"Whew. You'd scare off half your patients, and we would have to start letting the staff go."

He tilted her face toward his, caressed the delicate line of her jaw. "This is between you and me. What the rest of the world doesn't know won't hurt them."

"You sound very serious."

"I am. I don't like how we've gotten lost inside our lives, so I've come up with a plan to fix the problem. Are you in?"

She nodded.

"Then the first thing you have to do is trust me. So no making love on the first date. We need to build the tension."

"Wow. A sexy game."

Slipping an arm around her waist, he pulled her close and absorbed the feel of her—the only satisfaction he would get tonight. "A game with rules—like no pleasuring yourself."

"Those are fighting words."

Oh, yeah. "Who do you think will give in first?"

*There's even a question in your mind, silly man?*

"I don't know, Michael," she said aloud. "Guess it'll be fun to see."

He smiled. "Exciting, too."

"Yeah."

*And it just so happens that I'm in the mood to see you on your knees. This isn't going to be a one-way ride, Michael, not by a long stretch.*

He was counting on it.

"Then let the games begin." He couldn't resist sealing the deal with a kiss, and she melted against him, mouth parting in a soul-deep kiss.

A very promising start.

When they finally broke apart, they were laughing and breathless and a little awed by the thrill between them.

"We're going to have fun, Jilly my love. You have my word."

She gazed up at him with such promise in her eyes.

*Oh, Michael, after all this time...could you possibly have any idea how much I love you?*

Yes.

SERAFINE WAITED on the porch as Dr. Michael drove off into the night. She'd greeted him when he'd roared down the lane on Raphael's motorbike, but didn't ask how his night had gone. Had Mrs. Jillian been surprised? Serafine had wanted to know, but didn't want to be too obvious. Dr. Michael had looked pleased enough, and she decided that was a good sign.

As she watched the red brake lights wink and fade in the distance, she heard the screen door creak open behind her.

"You're torturing that man, Widow. He wants to know what you've done to him. You should put him out of his misery."

"Why are you up so late?" Ah, on second thought that question wasn't too hard to figure. "Couldn't sleep without knowing your motorbike came home safe and sound, could you?"

He only inclined his head.

"You'll make a good father one day, Raphael. You mark my words as truth."

"Suppose I've had enough practice."

"Lucky for your kin. They'll appreciate you proper one day. Mark that as truth, too. And I didn't tell Dr. Michael because the time's not right. He's still got work to do. A lot of work. I don't think he realizes it yet, but he will. I have faith."

Raphael bit back a reply and frowned, a look that was all her baby sister, brimming with piss and garlic. What was it about *knowing* that had always rubbed Virginie the wrong way?

"Dr. Michael asked us to clear out next weekend."

"You mean leave? All of us?"

Serafine nodded. "He's going to bring Mrs. Jillian up for the holiday."

"But why do we have to leave? This place is plenty big enough for all of us. I wanted to pull down that shower stall in Doll House. The wood's rotted. The door will probably fall off when someone's showering if I don't get it rebuilt before the campers come. Then we'll have a bunch of screaming girls."

"The Landrys can't relive their young memories if they're worried about running into one of us, now can they?"

"Got a lot of work to do around here. I think the Landrys should be more interested in seeing this place to rights in time for summer than reminiscing."

"I think we can help them manage both, don't you? Not as if they've been breathing down our necks to make sure our jobs are done proper. They're trusting us to do them right. The least we can do is give them a little space when they ask. We want this couple to work things out. Did you ever think about what would happen to this camp if the Landrys divorced?"

*That* won a scowl. "Well, I still say we got a lot of work to do and not all that much time left to do it in."

"Then get the stall tore out *this* weekend. It's only Friday."

"Ike wanted help rebuilding the pylons on the dock this weekend. He's afraid it won't hold up when the campers start pounding over it for the water-skiing classes. Doesn't want anyone getting hurt."

"Speaking of Ike, we need to invite him home for the big party. No one celebrates Memorial Day like the Baptistes, and that man spends too much time alone if you ask me."

"No one asked you, Widow, but if you ask me, I think you're sweet on the old coot. Don't think we all haven't noticed the way you keep showing up at the barn with your lunches and sending one of us down to his cabin with supper every night."

"I didn't ask you, did I?" Serafine sniffed. "And what's wrong with some good old Southern hospitality? Do unto others and all that."

Raphael's smirk irritated Serafine more than any answer might have.

"Pshaw, boy. Pay attention to your own business."

"What happens around Camp Cavelier *is* my business."

"Well, well. You seem to be settling in right comfy here, and your kin, too. Would think you'd want the owners of this place to be happy all the way around. Especially when they're proving so easy to work for."

"I do."

"Then what's the trouble?"

He shrugged. "Just doesn't feel right leaving."

"Why's that?"

"Maybe because the Landrys aren't around much. Maybe because we're the ones here all the time, it feels like we're abandoning things."

Serafine considered that. "I hear you, boy. You care, so you want to make sure things are cared for right."

"Yeah, guess so. I like Mrs. Jillian and Dr. Michael well enough, but they don't know that Ike is struggling to keep that sow feeding her runty piglet. They don't know to run the water clear before drinking because we just dug a new line."

"This place feels like home already, doesn't it?" She patted Raphael on the back and smiled what she hoped was a reassuring smile. "You should leave the Landrys a note with good instructions. They'll do what you ask. They care about this place, too, even if they don't have enough time to run it proper. They're doing a fair share by paying the bills and hiring us, don't you think?"

He considered that and finally nodded. "All right, Widow. We'll clear out for the weekend and invite Ike. I'll leave a note." Then he headed back inside.

"Sleep well, boy," she said.

"You, too."

Serafine would sleep like a baby because Virginie's brood was settling in better than she had a right to hope. Raphael cared so much it sounded as if he owned the camp…. Serafine smiled into the night.

Now there was an idea.

*Several days later…*

ONE FANTASY NIGHT on a motorcycle and some steamy foreplay in a dark theater had changed something fundamental between Jillian and Michael. He'd changed the rules of their relationship and, as a result, she wasn't sure what to expect from him. A certain sense of breathlessness crept into her days, as if she stood always poised on the edge waiting to see what he would do next. He'd been attentive and loving, but there'd been no hint of leather. No motorcycle.

And no sex in sight.

Or any mention of anything real.

Not their conflict over Camp Cavelier. Not any curiosity about her doctors' appointments.

Jillian tamped down her impatience, reasoning that Michael's fantasy plan would bring them closer and they'd ultimately get around to dealing with reality. She only had to be patient, to keep her thoughts focused on the efforts he made to improve their relationship and not on everything he wasn't doing. She couldn't allow these unresolved issues to gain momentum in her mind because she'd wind up resentful.

True, reality should rank above fantasy, and she was hurt that he hadn't asked anything about how things were going with her doctors' visits. But as she had chosen not to inform him of the problem, she could only fault him for inattentiveness.

Michael had said she needed to trust him, which meant trusting they'd eventually get around to the real stuff. When they did, she figured they'd be all the more ready to tackle the problems. She kept reminding herself of that whenever her impatience got the better of her.

And, fortunately, Michael's sexy games to build tension had proven a delightful distraction all weekend.

A titillating distraction that followed them from home to the clinic....

After escorting the day's first patients into exam rooms, Michael surprised her in the hallway. Clamping a hand over her mouth, he cut off any protest and crowded her into his office.

"What are you doing?" she asked when he finally let her go to flip the lock on the door.

Rounding on her, he captured her gaze with a bold stare, but didn't say a word, just eyed her as if anticipating the first bite of Widow Serafine's gumbo.

"Michael?"

"Trust me," was all he said, and before Jillian realized what he was about, he slid his hands beneath her smock.

Surprised, she instinctively pulled away, and her heart began to pound double-time.

"Shh," was all he said as he caught the clasp on her bra and snapped it open. Her breasts spilled into his hands.

"You want to make love? Now?"

She'd just seated three patients. If he didn't make an appearance in those exam rooms soon, his day would be completely fouled up before it even started.

"I always want to make love to you, Jilly. But I'm afraid we don't have time right now. I've got patients waiting."

"Then what are you—" She broke off sharply when he fished out a long silver chain from his lab coat pocket.

"Michael, what is that?"

He held up the chain for her perusal. It wasn't much of a stretch to put the padded clamps and her bare breasts together.

"Are those nipple clamps?"

He nodded.

She did *not* want to know where he'd gotten this sex toy. Just the thought of him shopping in one of Natchez's adult stores was enough to make her break a sweat. His SUV wasn't exactly nondescript with all its Mississippi Pride paraphernalia and tag that read: SMLE DR.

So she didn't ask, only watched, strangely fascinated as he tested a clamp. "Michael, are you expecting me to wear those?"

That answer was painfully obvious, and he must have recognized her rising disbelief because he slipped an arm around her waist and locked her against him.

"I'm going to make sure you're thinking about me this morning." His gaze twinkled, deep-blue lights that shone with his amusement, his arousal. "We're building tension, remember?"

"Does that mean you can wear them, too?"

His grimace made her laugh.

"You can dish it out, but you can't take it, can you, Michael?"

"Sure I can."

"We'll see."

"We will." Catching her nipple, he rolled it between his thumb and forefinger suggestively. Jillian gasped as every muscle in her body gathered tight in response to his touch.

His expression softened around the edges with that look he always got when they made love, right before he sank deep inside her, as if there was no place in the world he'd rather be. And beneath his knowing look she grew flustered. It was more than giddy, more than arousal. This was a feeling she remembered from long ago, a feeling that Michael believed she was his dream come true and the realization both pleased and awed him.

It pleased and awed her, too.

He was so intent on his sexy ministrations, rolling and squeezing her nipple until he could maneuver the padded clamp onto her aroused skin, that she grew unaccountably self-conscious, almost shy. Especially when he met her gaze, and eased the clamp shut.

Jillian held her breath, not surprised by his gentleness, but very surprised by the white heat that bolted through her. She sucked in a breath that shuddered raggedly between them.

"How's that feel?" he asked.

She just nodded.

"It's not too tight, is it? I don't want you to get numb. Sort of defeats the purpose."

Just when had he become an authority on sex toys?

"It's okay," she managed to say.

But the feeling was much more than okay. Sensation blasted through her, coiling deep inside and flooding between her thighs so intensely that she could barely breathe.

That seemed to content Michael because no sooner did

he let go of one clamp than he started up the process again with the other. Only this time Jillian sank back against the wall as he teased her nipple to life, suddenly so weak in the knees that she could hardly stand.

Did he really expect her to work like this?

Apparently so. He worked her nipple with more concentration than she'd ever seen him focus on a root canal. He teased and tugged until her nipple was swollen and erect. She'd had no clue he'd come up with sex toys to increase the tension. Then again, after the handcuffs and leather, she should have.

He applied the second clamp, the chain dangling between her bare breasts, only this time she had to bite her lip to keep from gasping. Sensation poured through her, so incredibly powerful, so deliciously decadent that she could only arch against the wall for support and hang on.

"That feels good?"

"Mmm-hmm." It was really all she could manage. Sensation wound through her, making it difficult to concentrate on anything but the heat. And when Michael gave a light tug on the chain dangling between her bare breasts, he started up a chain reaction that left Jillian's sex clenching so hard that she thought she might climax on the spot.

"Looks like you feel *really* good."

*There* was an understatement, but Jillian couldn't get the words out. She didn't have to, though. Michael already knew and stood leering down at her while enjoying the show.

He gave another tug on the chain, this time slower, longer, harder, until her nipples stretched, and her whole body answered. And to her amazement, Jillian did climax, right then and there, not a full-blown explosion, but a

delicate sprinkling of sensation that left her gasping for air
and the chain dangling wildly between her bare breasts.

Michael laughed. "Oh, I'm going to like this, Jilly. I'm
going to like this a lot."

If Jillian could have spoken, she would have said, "Me,
too."

*Later that week...*

MICHAEL PUT the finishing touches on another fantasy invitation. He set the printer into action then watched with
satisfaction as his latest creation sprang forth in full color.

He'd doctored a promotional photo of the camp's Lake
Lily to read:

> You are cordially invited for a weekend fantasy
> getaway at Camp Cavelier.

Michael had a fond memory of skinny-dipping in that lake
and hoped the reminder would inspire Jillian to more sexy
adventures. Around dealing with the farm chores, they'd
still have three nights and days to explore another fantasy.

The nipple clamps had been a big hit.

Michael had decided on cowboy gear this time. Chaps
and lassoes sounded much more romantic than boots and
gloves, though they would be playing farmhands to give Ike
the weekend off. Jillian wouldn't mind. Not even mucking
stables had ever dampened her enthusiasm for the outdoors.

Michael wasn't so enthusiastic about that part of the
fantasy, but he'd survive. *If* he survived until the weekend,
of course. Upping the tension was proving a mixed bag.

As was getting back into shape again, which had given him a surplus of energy. Combined with the dreamy look on Jillian's face every time he'd cornered her alone to surprise her with some new sexy gizmo, he'd been walking around just shy of hard since Monday.

He'd hoped to cut his daily swim short and lock himself inside his office to make this invitation. But that hadn't happened as he'd also needed a long stint in the cold water to calm his raging libido.

So, he wound up ducking out on a patient while Charlotte prepared a temporary crown.

Pleased with his effort, he folded the card, slid it inside an envelope and was about to go off in search of his wife when a knock on the door sounded. He swung it wide to find Jillian.

"I was just coming to look for—"

He didn't get another word out before Jillian brushed full against him and crowded him back inside his office. She kicked the door shut behind her and flipped the lock.

"Since you already left your patient stranded in your chair, I figured you wouldn't mind me taking a few minutes of your time."

"My time is all yours, my beautiful bride."

When she flashed a high-beam smile, he knew his response was exactly what she'd been hoping to hear.

Reaching for his hand, she pulled him closer. "I want to give you something to build the tension." With that she guided his hand under her smock then inside the waistband of her pants.

With her hand as a guide, he found his fingers grazing a smooth sweep of warm skin…down, down, down. "Jillian, you aren't wearing any panties."

A challenge blazed like amber fire in her eyes. She shook her head slowly. "No panties."

His fingers rounded the soft mound of her neatly shaved sex. He forged ahead even farther and moist, hot skin yielded beneath his touch.

Jillian shivered.

"And you're cleanly shaven, too."

"Very cleanly."

Now he shivered, all effects of a cold swim vanishing as his body went on red alert. "This is torture, you know?"

"I know." Pressing his hand to hold it still, she rocked her hips suggestively. "For both of us."

*You deserve to be tortured after what you've done to me. Monday—nipple clamps. Tuesday—a personal vibrator, and today...mmm, the stimulator spheres.*

Well, even if Michael could have admitted to hearing her thoughts, he couldn't exactly argue the point now, could he?

He shimmied his hand around and found the string to the modified ben-wa balls set that he'd gifted her with earlier. "I wondered if you'd take these out when I went to swim."

"You asked me not to."

"Yes, I did." Catching a finger around the dangling string, he tugged lightly, smiled when her expression softened and she melted against him.

"Oh." She sucked in the sound on a deep inhalation.

"Aroused?"

"Oh, yeah."

His crotch gave a warning throb. He wanted her. He wanted to forget all about building tension and shaking up their relationship.... He forced one hand from the danger zone and handed her his invitation.

Just enough of a distraction so he could breathe again.

"What's this?" she asked.

"Open it."

She slipped the invitation from the envelope, her eyes sparkling as she scanned the page. "You want to go away?"

"Made the arrangements already. Widow Serafine and her family are taking Ike down for the Baptiste family picnic."

"The camp will be all ours?"

He nodded. "We'll have to take care of the animals, but I didn't think you'd mind."

"Of course not." She threw her arms around his neck and pressed against him in a way that flooded his thoughts of what Jillian *wasn't* wearing under her uniform.

Sliding his hands along her bottom, he anchored her close, enjoying the feel of the soft fabric molding her tight cheeks, the pressure of the padded clamps he could feel through their clothing. His crotch reacted even more insistently, and Jillian laughed, noticing.

"You'd better control yourself. You've got patients waiting."

"How can I control myself when I know you're going commando?"

Now there was a question. One that obviously delighted Jillian because she tossed her head back, sending those glossy waves tumbling sexily over her shoulders, torturing him with thoughts of how his fingers would feel threading through all that cool silk.

"I thought you wanted to build the tension?" she asked dryly.

"I do. But we've got to make it until the weekend."

"Worried?"

"Very."

She grinned. "I'm flattered."

He sank his fingers into her bottom, anchoring her so he could rock his own hips to ease this ache. He shuddered.

She chuckled.

*I'm fighting fire with fire here, Michael. You'll be begging by Friday.*

"I had no idea you were so bloodthirsty." The words were out of his mouth before he thought the better of it.

Jillian only laughed, though, and he leaped in with a suggestion to cover his slip.

"Maybe we should have dinner to discuss this bloodthirsty streak of yours," he suggested. "I want to know why watching me suffer is turning you on."

"Mmm. For the same reason it turns you on, I'd guess. You like being able to make me squirm. Power is powerful stuff." She arched her body so his erection ground against her and dragged another shiver from him. "Think we can get out of here early enough tonight for dinner at a decent time?"

"We're squeezing life in around us, remember?"

She rocked against him again, clearly on edge and enjoying the feel of their bodies touching. Michael knew right then and there that he was in trouble. Friday was too far away.

And that thought, along with every melting glance she gave him, haunted Michael the rest of the afternoon. By the time he finished up his last patients of the day, he was mentally searching for a caveat in his tension-building clause.

"I hear you're taking Jillian to dinner," Charlotte said, pausing in the front doorway on her way out.

Michael nodded. "Kevin's."

"He should comp your dinner after standing you up for his last appointment."

"I told him a decent table and five-star service will square us."

Charlotte laughed. "Good for you. Then see you both bright and early tomorrow."

"Have a good night," Jillian said.

"Yeah," Michael added as Charlotte turned to head out the door.

She stopped at the last minute, though, and turned back to them. "Oh, Jillian. I forgot to tell you that Dr. Hyatt's office left a message on voice mail, confirming your appointment for tomorrow at 3:30."

"Thank goodness you picked up. I'd completely forgotten."

Michael didn't wonder why. Not when his beautiful bride had had other, much more pleasurable things to occupy her thoughts today. Namely the spheres that were currently jingling around inside her with every step she took.

Charlotte left and Michael locked the door behind her. "Ready, Jilly?"

"Just have to put the phones on service." She reached for the phone. "So, do I have to wear your latest gift to dinner?"

"That depends on—"

The telephone rang.

Last-second calls were never good. Jillian clearly knew it, too, and sat with her finger poised over the keypad, ready to depress the code to roll the phones over to the service. He could hear her thinking.

*Oh, no. We just can't catch a break, can we?*

"What do you want to do?" she asked him.

Michael stared at the phone in indecision, what Jillian said and what she thought waging a battle inside his head.

"Michael?"

He'd concocted this entire fantasy idea with the intention of making more time for the two of them. How could he have her pick up that phone?

How could he not?

Most offices closed at five. When someone called at five-oh-four, there was usually a reason. Question was: did he want to find out what that reason was now or hope the service didn't call with an emergency while he and Jillian were at dinner?

*My sweet Michael, I would never ask you to turn your back on a patient. Not even for a fantasy.*

She depressed the speaker button. "Dr. Landry's office. May I help you?"

"Oh, thank goodness," a female voice on the other end blurted. "I was afraid you'd left for the day."

The woman's relief blasted over the speaker, a nearly tangible force, and Michael saw all hope of their intimate dinner die a swift death.

"You caught us in the nick of time." Jillian didn't meet his gaze. "What's going on?"

The patient explained how she'd been watching her son's baseball game when the baseman's glove had flown off, hitting her full in the face and knocking out her front tooth.

"You've still got the tooth?"

"In a carton of milk. I didn't know if that's an old wives' tale but I wasn't taking any chances. I'm desperate." Her voice rose on every syllable like the whine of a straining fan belt. "I'm scheduled to speak to the entire Taylor supervisory conference at eight in the morning. All one hundred and six of them. I can't go on without a front tooth."

He tried to catch Jillian's eye for some hint about where she stood on this, but the chilling reality hit him full in the face, nearly hard enough to knock out a few of his own teeth.

He had no choice, not if he wanted to look himself in the mirror. "Come on in. I'll wait."

He disconnected the call. "I'm sorry, Jilly."

"Oh, Michael, don't be." She smiled one of those bittersweet smiles, and he knew she wouldn't have wanted him to leave any damsel in distress. "The fantasy has been wonderful, but we live real lives. I wouldn't have it any other way."

He believed her. But that didn't change the fact that he was letting his work get in the way of them, again. And her understanding shouldn't have made him feel worse, but it did. "This won't take too long, but we'll probably be too late for dinner."

"We'll go another night. Just do what you need to do."

Once again he'd be letting their time together take second place to his work. "You're sure?"

"Of course, I'm sure. Why would you even ask me that?"

Turning her attention back to the phones, she depressed the pass code to activate the service and ended the conversation.

Michael had asked because he felt bad. "I know you understand. It's just that I've been trying to change things, and here I am canceling our plans."

She glanced over the counter, warmth making her eyes seemed flecked with the same gold that spangled her lashes. "You *are* changing things. You might have to cancel, but usually you wouldn't think a thing about it. We'll get the focus back where it belongs. It'll just take time. And you have to work, Michael. Emergencies are going to happen. And I would never ask you to sacrifice your patients. I love your commitment to them."

*I just wish you felt as committed to me the rest of the time.*

Michael frowned. *That* statement seemed to come out of the blue and felt downright unfair. He had to fight back the urge to defend himself against her silent charges. How could he possibly be more committed? They lived together and worked together....

"You know I'm going stand beside you no matter what. That's what a good wife does."

*Even if you don't give me nearly as much thought as you do your patients. If you did, you might actually remember my birthday every once in a while.*

Something about that made her smile, and she wheeled the chair away from the desk to replace a file on the shelves. But she wasn't done thinking. Not by a long shot.

"Jillian, I know you're the *best* wife. You know that, don't you?"

"Of course I do."

*When you think about it—which I'd guess isn't often since you don't have a clue about what's going on in my life unless I inform you. You haven't even noticed me running between doctors to figure out what to do with this lump in my breast.*

Lump? What lump?

"And we're changing things," she said reassuringly. "That's what's important."

*You're even coming around about the camp. I know you didn't want to buy the place, but it was important to me. I wasn't asking you for much, just to help me out a little until I got some good people in place.*

"Jillian, I—"

"I love you, Michael. I'm willing to take things one step at a time." She rolled back to the desk. "Honestly."

*I honestly hope we can tackle the important stuff and make more time for us. Life's just passing us by. But I've been under a lot of pressure lately. Maybe I shouldn't expect so much. You've been so thoughtful with your fantasy. Maybe I should just let that be enough.*

Michael just stood there as Jillian handed him a file.

"Here's the chart. I'll go get everything ready in the back." She didn't give him a chance to reply, just pushed through the doorway and disappeared down the hall.

No, she wasn't expecting too much.

Michael was guilty as charged. He just hadn't realized it. He hadn't spent any time thinking about what was going on in Jillian's life until he'd been inadvertently dropped inside her head. He remembered her telling him about her doctor's appointment. He also remembered her telling him about a radiologist's appointment.

Charlotte had just mentioned another appointment, and it had never even occurred to him to ask her what was going on. He hadn't given a second thought to the fact that she was going to see her gynecologist again when she'd just told him she'd gone a few weeks ago.

He wanted to get angry that she hadn't told him these visits weren't routine. Especially when Charlotte seemed to know more than he did. But Jillian had done her part by informing him. Didn't he have a responsibility to take the next step and ask how things had gone?

No, she wasn't expecting too much at all.

He thought about her comments regarding the camp, and he couldn't deny her charges there, either, which upon reflection seemed like crappy treatment for the woman who'd devoted her life to him. When he thought about all the things she did: running his office, their home, their social and family lives....

Did he do anything else but work?

Jillian had given up a full ride to an Ivy League university so she could be with him at the college of *his* choice. She'd doubled her course load to get done in time to accompany *him* to dental school. She'd never applied for a job to use her business degree, even though he knew at least a dozen head-hunters had contacted her during her last semester.

She'd applied her skills to running *his* practice.

The only person Michael had to be angry at was himself—for not realizing more than their sex life needed his attention.

# 10

SERAFINE spread out the college scholarship forms over the kitchen table and sat back in the chair for a good look. She wasn't sure why she'd had the urge to pull out all this paperwork, but while she and Marie-Louise had been giving the owners' cottage a good scrubbing, the impulse to get back here had hit hard.

Serafine always followed her impulses. She *knew* she'd find out the why-for and how-for soon enough.

While perusing the fine print, she heard the screen door squeak open. Raphael and Philip appeared, looking grease-spattered and hardworking in their rumpled coveralls.

"Thought you boys were helping Ike fix that old tractor."

Philip headed for the refrigerator and grabbed a bottle of water. He tossed another to Raphael, who caught it one-handed. "We were, but we're all done."

"That was fast."

"Only needed to rebuild the carburetor," Raphael explained.

"Bet Ike was glad he didn't have to tote that old tractor down to the shop and saved Mrs. Jillian a pretty penny." Camp Cavelier kept offering up chances for the boys to prove their skills were a perfect fit. She figured Ike would share that information with Mrs. Jillian and Dr. Michael soon enough.

As far as Serafine was concerned, things couldn't be working out any better.

Raphael raised his water bottle in salute as he sidled toward the table for a peek. "What you got there?"

"Some college papers."

"College papers?" His gaze narrowed. "Who's going to college?"

"I was trying to figure out a way that you all might."

Raphael eyed her narrowly.

Philip blinked in surprise before demanding, "And how are we supposed to pull our weight around here and go to college?"

"You make it sound as if I'm asking you all to swim the Gulf to Texas."

"Aren't you, Widow?" Raphael asked.

"No. I'm not." Leaning back in the chair, she swept a hand over the table, gesturing to the papers spread out before her. Brochures. Applications. Various and sundry forms.

"These here are scholarship papers, boys. There's plenty of money available to send folks to school who want to go. This brochure here offers money for historic preservation. And this one here is for wildlife conservation. Camp Cavelier is historic and full of wildlife."

She didn't give them a chance to interrupt but forged on. "Since y'all are working for Mrs. Jillian and Dr. Michael, I'm betting we can convince them to pony up some money to train y'all to run this camp."

Silence followed. But Raphael wasn't arguing, and Serafine considered that a very good sign.

"You know Marie-Louise wants to go to college." She met Raphael's gaze. "And I know you've been trying to set aside some money so she can take some classes in the fall. Think you got enough yet?"

"How'd you know about that?"

She rolled her gaze heavenward. *Knowing* was what she did. That was no secret. "It's a good thing you're doing for your sister. So what'd you come up with?"

"I had enough for her first semester—if she went to the community college back in Louisiana. In Natchez, we're considered out of state until we've lived here for two years."

Serafine shook her head. "So now you've got a problem. Take a look at what I've got here. My head's not the best for numbers, but if we can get the Landrys' help, y'all could go to the university right here in Mississippi."

Philip plunked down into a chair, still clearly disbelieving, while Raphael circled the table, shooting wary glances at the various brochures. Serafine picked up one and forced it into his hand.

"Just take a look, boy."

"I barely made it through high school," Philip admitted. "What makes you think anyone would want to give me money to go to college?"

"You barely made it through high school because you were skipping classes to run with your gang of no-account friends. There's nothing wrong with your brain except that you haven't been using it." Serafine bopped him upside the head with the flat of her hand and earned a scowl. "You got a head for numbers. You hardly went to class at all, and you still got good marks in all your math classes."

"That's because math is easy."

Serafine chuckled. "For you, maybe. If you start classes and prove you can use the brain the good Lord gave you, I'm betting you could earn some of that scholarship money for yourself."

"What makes you think Mrs. Jillian and Dr. Michael will go for something like this?" Raphael asked, still prowling around the table.

"I just *know*. Mrs. Jillian only bought this camp because it's part of Natchez history. She's big into her historic causes—Dr. Michael told us that. I've been reading up on all that Internet information Raphael printed about the camp and got to thinking...with Marie-Louise's talent for cooking and caring for people, she could study hospitality management.

"Raphael, you've been in charge of this bunch since your granny died. You're a shoo-in for running the camp. Maybe you could get a business management degree. And, Philip, with your head for numbers, you could study accounting and handle the camp's finances. That would save Mrs. Jillian from running back and forth to her accountant with every receipt. Should be that she only needs a tax man at tax time, don't you think? Or maybe not at all. Between the three of you and Ike to handle the farm, seems to me this place would be well cared for."

Both boys stared at her as if she'd grown a second head, but Serafine held her tongue to let her words sink in.

"Sounds to me like you're trying to bully these nice people into giving up their camp, Widow," Raphael said, but there was something more in his voice than accusation. Something…*hopeful.* "Me and my kin won't be a part. The Landrys are nice people, and they're being good to us."

"Of course they are, which is exactly why we're here. Your loyalty is well placed, but the Landrys don't have time to run this camp—not full-time, anyway. That's why they hired us. And don't you remember Dr. Michael saying he wanted kids?"

"He said that to *Mrs. Jillian.*"

"But he said it loud enough for us to hear."

"He didn't know you were eavesdropping."

Philip snickered and Serafine shot him a quelling frown that shut him up quick.

"Hear me out, boys," she said. "Camp Cavelier has always been owned by a family. Dr. Michael and Mrs. Jillian might be pinch-hitting so the camp doesn't get sold and the land developed, but they don't seem all that eager to give up their careers. Mrs. Jillian said she wants strong people to run this place. I'm guessing if she's convinced there's a family who might be capable of taking over, she might help that family train up proper for the job.

"Who knows what'll happen down the road? But it seems to me like this might work out all the way around. You're a family that needs a home. This camp is a home that needs a family. The Landrys bought the place as a labor of love. Did you ever think they might have done that just to make sure it's safe until the right family came along?" She shrugged. "Since we're heading home for the celebration this weekend, I figure it might be a good time to talk with Philly Bananas."

"Philly Bananas?" Philip exchanged a puzzled look

with Raphael. "What do we want to be talking to him about all this?"

"He's a lawyer."

"Business law, Widow," Raphael pointed out.

"Well, we're looking to conduct business with the Landrys." To Serafine's knowledge no one in New Iberia Parish had ever discovered why the boy named Phillip Boudreaux had been so fond of bananas that he'd actually become known by the name, but she *knew* the man he'd grown into could help. "He'll write us up something legal to show our commitment to this place. Maybe there's some sort of contract you can sign that'll guarantee you'll stay working here if the Landrys let you use the camp to get some of those scholarships. You know, something that makes it official. To let them know you're looking for a future here."

"It's worth a shot, Raphael," Philip said. "We got nothing else to do."

"Are you saying you're willing to tackle school?" Raphael shot him a skeptical glance.

"Hell, why not? I'm tired of sitting around feeling useless while I watch you bust your ass keeping us together. I like it around here. I like Ike. I like fixing things. I like that Marie-Louise is singing again. Didn't you notice how she bakes more desserts when she's singing?"

Serafine held her tongue and let fate play its hand.

Raphael shot her a look as if she'd cast a magic spell on his baby brother. But he didn't give her one word of sass. Nope, he pulled out a chair, sat down and said, "All right, Widow, why don't you show us what you got here."

*On approach to the big weekend*

JILLIAN HAD a decision to make. Her gynecologist had pulled some strings and sent her directly upstairs to a surgeon in the same office building, who was a friend of his. Both men consulted and agreed that her lump, which appeared to be a fibroadenoma, must come out.

She was comfortable with the plan of action and their reassurances that the mass was likely benign. But only a biopsy would confirm that. All her research supported exactly what the doctors were telling her, and Dr. Hyatt had been her gynecologist since she'd been seventeen years old. She trusted his opinion.

Now she had to let Michael know she was facing a surgical procedure, but she didn't want to spoil their weekend.

Should she wait until afterward to tell him? Or tell him before? Either way, she would force the issue. She'd have to be honest about her feelings, which would leave him reacting with some feelings of his own. Especially when she realized how long this had been going on and that she hadn't told him. He'd likely feel angry she hadn't said anything and guilty because he hadn't asked. And definitely worried.

They'd eventually work through all the emotions, but this wasn't the best scenario for a fantasy weekend.

It was as she was leaving the doctor's office that Jillian came up with plan C.

Michael had been using sexy games as a distraction from reality, and playing his sexy games had done exactly what he'd intended, along with building their sexual tension to a fever pitch. By the time the weekend arrived, they'd be primed and ready for sex.

Why shouldn't she use that to her advantage?

If she played her cards right, lots of wonderful lovemaking could soften the blow of her news enough to open up some new lines of communication between them. Maybe it was time for her to take the situation firmly in hand. She'd played things his way. Now it was her turn.

And she knew exactly where to go for help.

To the mall.

She had a friend who managed a lingerie franchise. Stephanie had been Jillian's best friend in high school. While their lives had taken them in directions that didn't often bisect, they stayed in touch—if not frequently, then at least regularly enough to have some clue of what was happening in each other's lives.

Jillian had barely made it through the front door of Alexandria's Whisper, an upscale lingerie shop that catered to women in a discreetly decadent atmosphere, before a salesperson recognized her and called the store manager. By the time she'd reached the pajama displays, she found Stephanie hurrying toward her. She swept through the racks of sheer nothings, looking chic in a cocoa silk suit that complemented her bright red hair and the clear skin that had once been the envy of her teammates.

"Jillian, it's so good to see you." Stephanie gave her a big hug, and they caught up on family and work.

"As soon as I heard you and Michael had bought Camp Cavelier, I told Bob he'd better sell off a few cows because I'm sending both kids for the whole summer, *every* summer." Stephanie laughed the same good-natured laugh that had often gotten her teammates busted after curfew while traveling to competitions. "At least I know you'll make sure my kiddos get assigned good cabins. Not like that year we were in Fan Attic. Still can't figure out what we did to tick off Bernice."

"Oh, it wasn't that bad. And I don't think we did anything. It was an honest scheduling mistake. She assigned us to Doll House the following year."

"In time for Michael to surprise us with snakes. Lucky us."

Jillian winced. Even the passage of time hadn't dulled *that* memory. "He's been making up for it ever since. Trust me."

"So that's why you married the guy." Stephanie rolled her eyes. "Now tell me what brings you by today? As much fun as it is to catch up, I know you're here for a reason."

Jillian cast a glance around and dropped her voice to a whisper. "Michael's taking me away for the weekend. I want to get something special to wear."

Stephanie arched an eyebrow skeptically. "*Not* your typical garden-variety undergarments in natural, white and black cotton."

Those garden-variety undergarments might be plain, but the lack of embellishment never seemed to affect the price. Jillian kept that opinion to herself. "Something special."

Emphasis on the *special*.

Understanding dawned on Stephanie's face. "Then you've come to the right place. Alexandria's Whisper does special, and you're talking to the queen. Tell me about your weekend."

"Think outdoorsy. Mountain cabin. Hills and streams. A whole glorious weekend under the stars."

"You're a piece of work, my friend. Most women would want a weekend at the Peabody, and you're stockpiling sexy nothings for a hiking trip in the woods."

"Different is what makes the world go 'round."

"Tee-hee." Stephanie led her on a tour of store displays while discussing the merits of what might be considered special for an outdoorsy weekend.

Eyeballing corset bras and thongs with Stephanie turned out to be nothing like shopping for garden-variety undergarments in natural, white and black. Her friend had a provocative suggestion for everything, including the fishnet stockings and leather bustier that Jillian wouldn't even consider trying on.

"I said outdoorsy, Stephanie. Not dominatrix."

"You've lived a sheltered life. Did anyone ever tell you that?"

"Only you."

By the time Stephanie was juggling enough hangers to warrant a visit into a dressing room, she'd had Jillian not only blushing, but wondering how she'd ever made it into management of this upscale chain with such a raw sense of humor.

"Need my help?" Stephanie asked.

"Thanks. I'll call if I do."

"Suit yourself. But you have my word I won't tell the girls which of your parts are still real and which aren't. It's an oath we lingerie ladies take. Strict client confidentiality."

"I'm sure."

With a laugh, Stephanie disappeared, pulling the door shut behind her.

Jillian situated herself inside the cushy dressing room and undressed, smiling at the sight of her garden-variety bra and panties—in natural today.

After a quick perusal of the items Stephanie had organized on the wall rack, Jillian decided to start with a tasteful pink satin babydoll. She slipped the clingy outfit on to find that the bodice was padded for some lift 'em and separate 'em action, so far from the comfy cotton shorts sets she normally slept in that she just might give Michael a heart attack.

Or herself. She didn't even recognize her own reflection in the clingy outfit.

Whoever had said the packaging could make all the difference hadn't been kidding.

She tried not to stare, tried to be objective about the way she looked, but couldn't help grinning like a fool. She was a woman on a mission.

Michael, watch out.

She remembered this feeling. A sense of daring that grew the longer she stared in the mirror. A knowledge that she possessed the power to bring Michael to his knees.

This feeling had once been a normal part of her days. Once upon a time, her first waking thoughts had been about Michael. When she closed her eyes to sleep, she'd nestle against him and feel as if everything in her world was right. No problem was too big when they were together. No obstacle insurmountable.

When was the last time she'd dressed to entice her husband?

Jillian honestly couldn't remember, but she remembered the last time Michael had dressed to entice her.

When he'd shown up on a motorcycle in leather.

And this would be her reply. Sure, she enjoyed the security of knowing that Michael still appreciated her when she crawled into bed with her hair in a knot and moisturizer all over her face. But if she wanted passion in her marriage then she had to make time to be passionate.

It was all so simple, really.

Life was too short to waste precious time. She'd come face to face with that realization today while viewing her films and feeling grateful she wasn't facing chemo and radiation.

So, Jillian renewed her determination to make the weekend special. She'd make love to her husband and break her news as easily as possible and maybe, just maybe, Michael would feel the same way, too. She really did miss him.

She tried on a flirty little outfit that left nothing to the imagination. Short shorts that were really no more than a scrap of fabric draped on her hips, decadent for the straps that would affix to silky hose. She wasn't entirely sure how silky hose would hold up in the camp, but the look was so erotic that she decided to give it a go anyway.

Twirling in a slow circle, she savored the sight of the soft, stretchy lace molding her curves, a sight both familiar and decadently unfamiliar.

"How'd we do?" Stephanie asked when she finally emerged, dressed back in her garden-variety undies, but with an attitude that was anything but garden-variety.

"They're perfect."

Stephanie's eyes widened. "All of them?"

Jillian nodded, laughing when her friend gave a low whistle and said, "That's the right idea. You go, girl."

But as Jillian signed the credit card receipt, she realized she'd been wrong about something after all. At Alexandria's Whisper, lack of embellishment apparently did keep the cost down. *Way* down.

MICHAEL HAD DECIDED against asking Jillian about how her doctor's appointment had gone. The more he thought about what had been happening with Jillian's health, the more he realized that all the strife over Camp Cavelier was a symptom of the real, even bigger problem—his.

He'd been completely oblivious to Jillian—about more than her health. Camp Cavelier seemed to be the straw that had broken the camel's back.

Given his insider information, he'd decided against grilling her with questions until they could discuss his negligence and what he could do not to be shut out anymore.

This wasn't a conversation that could take place in the car on the way home from work. This was a conversation that would have to happen this weekend when he had ample opportunity to convince her he was worthy of her trust again, *after* he figured out how he might do that.

He hadn't been acting very worthy.

And that truth never hit so hard as when he faced the rest of the week without knowing what was happening with her health.

He considered calling her gynecologist but knew the privacy laws would prevent the release of any information without Jillian's written consent.

Professional courtesy might have yielded up some answers, except the simple act of asking would reveal that his wife hadn't shared the information and would place her doctor in the gray area of liquid ethics.

Michael would not treat himself to another question-and-answer session with Charlotte under any circumstances. He didn't need to read her mind to know his questions would only yield up another, "Why are you asking me? Go ask your wife."

But Michael couldn't sleep without knowing, so after

Jillian went to bed, he began a search for information. If he knew his wife, she'd have some sort of paper trail.

And she did—in a yellow medical folder on top of the file cabinet beside the fax machine.

Michael wondered how long the file had been sitting there. He vaguely recalled noticing it before, and, knowing Jillian, she'd been carrying it back and forth with her, adding reports and films after each of her appointments.

It hadn't once occurred to him to pick it up or to even ask her about it.

Her name had been printed with black permanent marker across the front with her birth date and social security number. He knew those numbers by heart, a privilege he'd earned when he'd married her.

But being informed about what was happening in her life was also a privilege—one he obviously hadn't earned lately.

So Michael stood there with that medical file in his hands, the sounds of his house settling for the night feeling strangely unfamiliar. The chime of the grandfather clock striking one-thirty. The whir of the air conditioner as the fan cycled on. The unbroken quiet where the inhabitants were asleep. Or should have been.

The simple fact that Jillian had left this folder out in the open suggested that she wasn't concealing anything. No, likely she'd known he wouldn't pay any attention to it. The blame was his. He'd been oblivious and totally self-absorbed, so she'd excluded him from this part of her life.

*You don't have a clue about what's going on in my life unless I inform you.*

She'd chosen not to inform him.

Why?

When he actually thought about it, Michael didn't find that such a hard question to answer.

She'd been worried. Since he hadn't made himself accessible to her, *informing* him would have made her feel too needy, when, to deal with her worry, she'd needed to take control.

She had. As he skimmed through the folder he noticed copies of reports labeled: Personal, Primary, Gynecologist, Surgeon. She was overseeing the passage of information between the doctors' offices. A meticulous office manager, Jillian understood the process and its pitfalls. She'd clearly decided she wouldn't allow her treatment to suffer by fate.

Her original mammogram was dated April. After the lump had been discovered, her gynecologist had sent her back to the radiologist for an ultrasound, then to a surgeon today.

Solid mass with clearly defined edges.

Both doctors were in agreement that the mass was likely a benign fibroid tumor and all had recommended the same treatment: lumpectomy and biopsy.

Only as he read the probable prognosis did Michael exhale, release the breath that had felt locked inside his chest. The procedure would be relatively easy; likely handled in the one-day surgery facility at the hospital.

Knowing his efficient wife, he searched through the paperwork to see if Jillian had scheduled the procedure, but he found no appointment card. He dug out the day planner from her briefcase and flipped through the calendar. Jillian hadn't written anything, so he was pretty sure she hadn't scheduled the surgery yet.

He should have felt relieved he hadn't missed that, at least, and had to wonder if she'd planned to tell him before the procedure. Surely he would have thought to question her if she'd scheduled a full day out of the office.

Michael wasn't willing to bet money on the answer.

He also remembered the advice Charlotte had given him.

*If you're waiting around for her to ask for your help or support, then you'll be waiting forever.*

Had she been warning him?

Viewed in this new light the exchange suddenly made sense. Charlotte knew Jillian had been leaving the office to see the doctor and had probably asked about the outcome.

Jillian had probably shared what was going on. No big secret. Just simple consideration.

Had he always been this oblivious, so wrapped up in himself that he took the woman he loved for granted?

Yes. That answer he would have bet money on.

Returning the reports to the folder and the day planner to Jillian's briefcase, he wondered if he could repair the damage he'd done to their relationship. How did he ask her to forgive him when he wasn't even sure if he could forgive himself?

Another answer he needed.

Michael's thoughts raced. He didn't feel remotely tired, but he headed into the bedroom and climbed into bed, the simple act of slipping beneath the warm covers helping to anchor him. Jillian exhaled softly as he wrapped himself around her. He inhaled the familiar scent of her hair.

Then he held her, just held her.

# 11

*The big day arrives*

WHEN JILLIAN opened her eyes, still feeling far too sleepy to face the day, a spray of bright color filled her vision. She blinked, forcing her gaze on what turned out to be a bouquet of gladioli propped on the floor beside the bed. There had to be three dozen in a tall crystal vase, all vibrant colors, all in perfect bloom, from the fist-sized blossoms on the bottom to tighter buds on top.

She smiled. Today was Friday, and it appeared that Michael intended their fantasy weekend to start even before they left for the camp.

"I thought I heard your alarm go off." He appeared in the doorway. He was carrying a cup of steaming coffee and came to a standstill, a smile playing across his mouth as he watched her. "Good morning."

"The flowers are gorgeous. Thank you."

"Glad you like them." He held up the cup. "I wanted to start your day off special."

"You have." Nestling back against the pillows, she snuggled beneath the warm covers and closed her eyes, perfectly content.

Her plan was in place, and in this drowsy state of half-sleep, she had every hope that they would segue from fantasy to reality during the weekend, weather the transition and come out stronger on the other side. After all, that's what marriages did—transitioned and changed and grew.

The mattress sank beneath Michael's weight, but she didn't open her eyes. Instead she savored the sleepy intimacy of the moment, feeling the promise about what the day, and the weekend, ahead would bring.

He ran a hand over her hair, a simple whisper of touch that made her feel cherished, appreciated.

"Do I get to look forward to various and sundry sex toys today?"

"Depends."

"On what?"

"How much you want me."

The fingertips he caressed along her cheek made her body tingle to life. "Guess I won't need any then. Tomorrow maybe."

"Fair enough."

She finally cracked an eyelid and peered up at him, caught him sipping from her cup. He looked freshly showered and oh, so handsome with his damp hair and cheeks slightly pink from a shave. "I like this, Michael."

"Waking up to flowers or coffee in bed?"

"Both. Neither. I like that we're paying attention to each other again."

"Me, too." He rustled his fingers through her hair, a playful gesture that made her smile. "I love you, Jilly."

"I love you, too."

He gazed down at her with his heart glowing in his

eyes, and Jillian couldn't remember being more hopeful. She needed to accept that life wasn't meant to be perfect all the time and needed to remember moments like these to stay focused on what was truly important—she and Michael living life together.

A *real* life, filled with ups and downs and fantasy.

The reminder was the wonderful start to a wonderful day.

Even work went uncharacteristically smoothly, as if everyone who came through the door was looking forward to the long weekend. Michael didn't run into any emergencies, so he stayed on schedule all day. The patients were in and out without lots of waiting, which kept everyone pleasant and cordial.

As Charlotte had been privy to Jillian's worries, she considered their upcoming weekend away a very good sign. During the day, every time Jillian turned a corner, Charlotte would roll her eyes and mouth the words, "Brandi, right."

Jillian even made peace with that one. The Speedo comment would dissolve into unimportance, for she wouldn't let doubt into her marriage again. Not when she'd been so off base about what had been going on in Michael's head.

An affair.

And he seemed determined to do it up right. Claiming that he'd get plenty of exercise mucking stalls over the weekend, he skipped his daily swim, and surprised Jillian with a trip to her favorite Chinese restaurant for lunch. They feasted on egg rolls and wonton soup and chatted about their plans for the weekend.

The tension built.

They'd decided to leave for the camp directly after closing the office, so the car was already packed for the trip. Ike called Jillian's cell phone just as Michael was pulling onto the highway to say that he and the Baptistes were heading out. He told her that he and Raphael had worked up a detailed list of instructions and made her promise to call if they ran into any trouble. They could be back in a matter of hours.

"You all go have fun, Ike," she told him. "If we have any questions, we'll call."

He seemed satisfied, and she disconnected, feeling as if everything about the camp was finally falling into place.

"Well, here we are," Michael said when he finally wheeled off the main road down the dirt path leading to the camp. "Raphael and Philip did a nice job on the sign."

Jillian wasn't sure what pleased her more—the sign or the fact that Michael noticed. "A far cry from the one that's been there all these years. They copied the logo from the Web site. Decided the camp needed a more professional image."

"They're an interesting bunch."

"That's for sure. Talented and hardworking. Ike's really happy with them, and that's a huge load off my mind. Now if I can just keep them happy so they stay."

Michael cast a sidelong glance. "Worried?"

She shrugged. "Widow Serafine is a long way from home. I just wonder if she'll be content here after her family is done rebuilding from the hurricane."

"Raphael, Philip and Marie-Louise are her family, too, and they obviously weren't happy in the bayou."

"I know. But they're all so young yet. They could decide to go to school or get married—"

"They can do all that and still work here. They want to work together, remember? The camp seems a good fit."

"Fingers crossed." And toes, too. She needed the Baptistes to help Ike handle the camp. She didn't want to place any more camp stress between her and Michael, not when they still hadn't come to any sort of real resolution yet.

But she had the weekend ahead to circle around to reality. After she seduced him senseless, she'd force them to address the issues. And she felt positive they'd tackle them head-on.

After all, Michael's fantasy weekend proved he was slowly making peace about the camp, didn't it?

He drove straight to the owners' cabin, where she found that someone—the Baptistes, she presumed—had planted bright impatiens in all the beds up front.

"That was so thoughtful," she said, delighted.

Michael smiled. "Especially because I never thought of that when we were coming up with ways to make this place habitable."

Jillian had known Michael would have spoken to Widow Serafine to make the arrangements for the weekend, but the very thought that he'd been so involved with the details of making their stay pleasant and comfortable came as another surprise.

She usually took care of the details.

"I'm sure it will be fine, Michael. A little rustic maybe…and we can always renovate someday if we want."

When he didn't reply, Jillian let the matter drop. She wasn't going to push, not yet. Not until she'd debuted a few of her sexy new outfits and had the man on his knees.

"We made it," he said, wheeling the SUV into a spot in front of the porch.

She reached for the house keys on the console between them, but he grabbed them first.

"Allow me." He opened the door and got out. "Hang on. I'll get yours."

She waited, liking that she was being treated to Michael's full gentleman mode. She accepted his hand to get out of the car, but no sooner did she stand than he leaned over and caught her against him. He swung her up into his arms.

"Michael!" She laughed, tossing her arms around his neck to hang on. "You're going to hurt your back."

"I'm fit now, or haven't you noticed?"

His butt was looking even better than it had in high school, and she couldn't wait to get him naked to prove it. "Couldn't miss it."

That seemed to please him. "Besides, I don't want you to be disappointed that I didn't pick you up on a motorcycle."

"I liked how you looked in leather, but I don't think I'd have enjoyed that trip on the back of a motorcycle."

"And where would we have put the garment bags?"

"There is that." She chuckled, plucking the keys from his hand to unlock the front door, not entirely trusting that he wouldn't drop her no matter how tight his butt was.

Then Michael turned sideways to scoot inside.

"Ohmigosh," she gasped. "This place looks so—"

"Refreshed?"

"You had Widow Serafine do all this?"

"Actually I asked Raphael to see what he could do. You mentioned remodeling before. He checked the place over and told me what needed to be done. Looks like he and

Philip can handle mostly everything. Said we'd only need to hire out some of the electrical and plumbing jobs because of the permits."

"Wow." Jillian wasn't sure what to make of this, but her heart started to pound a little harder. "Sounds like you've been talking to Raphael quite a bit."

"Yeah, I wanted to make sure that he and Philip checked to see if everything was working properly. Can't have a fantasy weekend without decent plumbing. But I asked Widow Serafine and Marie-Louise to spruce the place up. Make sure things were clean and whatnot."

New upholstery covers in shades of pine and gold concealed Bernice and Carl's worn-in furniture. There were new rugs on the plank floors, which had been waxed to a high gloss, and wood-slat blinds on the windows. The dining-room table not only had a lace cloth but an arrangement of colorful wildflowers.

"Mission accomplished," she said. "I'm seeing all sorts of possibilities. We can make this place great. I'll bet that knocking out a wall or two will rework the floor plan—"

"No reality, Jilly. We're all about fantasy right now, remember. That's the rule." Michael let her down, sliding her full length against him, all warm and hard and reminiscent of the tension that had been building this week.

"Still determined to see how long we can hold out?" She snuggled up against him suggestively. "I obviously haven't been trying hard enough if you still want to play by the rules when we have the camp to ourselves."

"Oh, you've been trying just fine. Trust me." He stared at her with such a smoldering gaze that her breath caught hard.

"I do, Michael." She felt that feeling again, that glow of knowing she could bring this man to his knees.

And would.

MICHAEL KNEW he was in trouble the second he tracked down Jillian in the stables. She'd gone off with Ike and Raphael's instructions to check on the animals while he'd been unpacking their garment bags. He'd asked her to wait, but she'd only laughed and headed out the door. She'd been thinking, though.

*Catch me if you can, Michael.*

He'd catch her all right, and she'd quickly find out their weekend wasn't going to be all about fun and games.

Michael had to restore Jillian's faith in him. Or at least get her to believe he'd recognized the real problem and was committed to fixing it.

She expected fantasy, so he'd begin by pleasuring her until she couldn't think straight. But he wouldn't make love to her. Not until he laid all his cards on the table. He intended to prove he was interested in more than just sex and convince her he wanted to share in all the areas of her life.

He'd address her health issues, explain what he knew and ask her to share the rest. He'd ask her to share how she felt about him not being there for her.

Because he hadn't been. He'd been wrapped up in his own world of contentment and complacency, thinking only about himself and his wants.

This weekend would be a fresh start.

But the instant Michael stepped foot inside the stable, he knew holding off on making love might be a problem.

*His* problem. And it looked like a *big* one.

Jillian speared hay into the stalls with a pitchfork, wearing nothing but a sexy shorts set that clung to her curves and left her long legs bare.

Michael stopped in the doorway, suddenly not feeling quite so comical in his cowboy duds. At least he wasn't the only one in costume. Under any other circumstances he might have laughed at the sight she made, such an odd blend of mouth-wateringly sexy and so totally under-dressed for the job, but the blood drained to his crotch so fast he felt dizzy.

Long toned legs that had captivated him the first time he'd ever seen them and had kept his attention ever since.

She looked like sex.

Every time she leaned over for another fork of hay, her clingy short shorts rode up her backside to reveal the tempting curve of her cheeks.

He flipped the brim of his Stetson up for a better view.

Damn, but she was even hotter today than she'd been when they'd first started dating. Her golden-red waves tumbled down her back as she hoisted another forkful, drawing his gaze to the lingerie molding her trim waist and giving enticing peeks of smooth skin whenever she lifted her arms.

When he saw her strolling through the office every day, he never forgot the lush body she kept primly hidden beneath her work uniform. When she ran around the house in various states of undress, he always appreciated the beauty that had guys all through high school and college going ape shit to steal her away. And when she'd dressed to the nines for Jenny Talbot's wedding, he'd been so proud that she'd been on his arm.

But Jillian was so much more than gorgeous. Did he spend nearly as much time thinking about the woman who handled his life? The strong, brilliant, competent woman who took on running Camp Cavelier in addition to all her other irons in the fire? What about the incredible woman who'd planned a seduction around caring for a stable filled with animals?

How could he overlook the amazing woman she was?

*I've got to get these horses fed and watered before Michael shows up. He's been working so hard all week. I don't know when he's found time to arrange this fantasy, but I want this weekend off to the right start.*

Here was something else that was going to change. Jillian was thinking about his needs and making excuses for his behavior, rationalizing the way he hadn't been helping her out as he should.

When did he think about her needs? She'd been working as hard as he had this week, likely even harder. She'd been dealing with her doctors, the camp, his practice, and obviously she'd gone shopping to prepare for their weekend.

"Don't you look sweet enough to eat?" he said.

She spun toward him, glossy hair flying around her face and neck, making her look like a vision.

"Well, hey there, cowboy." Her bold smile made the blood pulse between his legs.

"So what can I do to help, pretty lady?"

"Just stand there and look yummy. I need to give these guys water then I'll be all done in here."

Michael strode inside, feeling cocky as hell in his hand-tooled boots and Stetson. He must have looked cocky, too, because the color rode high on Jillian's cheeks.

She looked like a woman who knew he thought she looked yummy herself.

Grabbing the hose, he watered the horses, not minding the job one bit. Not when it left him to enjoy Jillian with fresh eyes, and not just how hot she looked in her sexy lingerie.

Jillian started shoveling with a vengeance now, so fast, in fact, that her skin began to glisten with a fine sheen of perspiration. Hairs clung to her temples and cheeks, curling sexily and drawing his thoughts to the way all her slick skin would feel naked against him.

He headed toward the trough. "You look hot, beautiful."

She shot a gaze back over her shoulder, warm eyes sparkling with her exertion, cheeks flushed and smile wide. "That's because you look so good."

Michael liked this awareness between them. She was something feeding horses dressed like a lingerie model, unafraid to get her hands or her sexy outfit dirty.

And Michael liked how she reacted to his awareness.

She flirted back.

Chuckling, he remembered how much he'd once enjoyed flirting with this woman.

So why had they ever stopped?

Holding her gaze, he adjusted the nozzle from the hose to a gentle stream. When she turned around to spear the pitchfork into the bale, he moved in to let the water pour down her back.

"Michael!" Jillian went rigid and dropped the pitchfork, but the damage was already done.

Water drenched her filmy lingerie until it clung to her like dew, rendering it practically see-through. He raised the hose so the stream sluiced down her front, molding her firm breasts in an erotic display, her nipples becoming rosy blushes of color and tight tips through the sheer fabric.

"Michael, I'm all wet."

"At least it's water and not baby snakes."

She made a strangled sound, but he didn't give her a chance to protest. Dropping the hose inside the trough, he slid his hands around her. "I love the feel of you wet and naked."

"I'm not naked."

He smiled at her breathlessness and helped himself to a handful of her full breasts veiled in wet silk. He pulled her back against him. "You will be, sugar."

That made her laugh. "I'm getting you all wet. And my grossly expensive sandals are soaked."

He ground his crotch against her so she wouldn't miss the effect she was having on him. "I'm not worried about your sandals. I'll buy you a new pair."

*Problem solved then. Until he sees what they cost.*

Michael made a mental note not to look at the price tag and fondled his warm handfuls, loving the feel of her.

She let her eyes flutter shut and relaxed against him. "Mmm. That feels so good."

Sounded like a request to him, so Michael indulged her, kneading her soft skin, exploring the curves, amazed that such simple touches could evoke such pleasurable responses—from both of them.

He pinched her nipples, rewarded when she arched up into his touch, making him feel the way he always did when he pleasured her.

Right.

She exhaled a sigh that echoed through the stable, making a horse whinny as if the poor guy had noticed the action taking place right outside his stall. She lifted her arms and draped them around his neck, making the skimpy top ride up her smooth stomach and treating him to even better access.

God, he loved this woman.

He didn't want any more distance between them, and he'd do whatever it damn well took to bridge the distance he'd created between them already. He hated the thought of her facing doctors and health issues alone. He hated her feeling as if she was all alone dealing with the responsibility of the camp.

But she had been, and he felt ashamed at his inattentiveness, his total self-absorption.

But behavior was changeable, and he refused to waste another second of their time together, not one instant when they could be exploring new interests—both hers and his. He wanted to live a real life with her, explore reality and fantasy.

If Jillian wanted him in leather, then, hell, he'd wear leather. If seeing him in cowboy boots and a Stetson turned her on, then he'd play her cowboy both in and out of bed.

She was his fantasy woman in her skimpy wet outfit.

And he was the *only* man for her. Always had been. And a lifetime together didn't seem like long enough. Not *nearly* long enough when she rocked her hips back and forth, riding the bulge in his pants.

*I know what you're trying to do here, cowboy, and if you think you're going to distract me, think again.*

Those were fighting words, so Michael dragged his hands down to her waist, pulled her impossibly closer until her cheeks parted around the bulging erection trapped inside his jeans.

She gave a soft moan as he braced his legs apart and tucked her close against his body so he could reach the mound of her sex that these wet short shorts didn't come close to hiding.

Distracting her.

Rocking her hips in sexy rhythm, she kneaded his erection to aching fullness. He wanted nothing more than to pop his fly open and make love to her right here in the hay.

But he was a man on a mission, and that mission was all about pleasuring Jillian.

Her bottoms were so short that all he had to do was nudge aside the fabric to find everything he wanted to touch. With one hand, he separated her moist skin. With the other, he began all the moves that soon had her quivering in his arms, those full-bodied shivers that made him smile.

*Oh...my...goodness. And he expects me to stand?*

Michael appreciated the warning. Bracing his legs wider, he supported her when she went boneless against him, riding his hand with smooth strokes, her breasts rising and falling temptingly on her shallow breaths.

She was amazing in her passion. Generous. Eager. He'd always loved that about her. She was an adventurous lover, as accommodating in bed as she was out of bed.

And Michael made the vow right then and there that he would never again take her for granted. He wouldn't waste another chance to show her how very much he loved her, how much he wanted her....

And he wanted her with a need he could barely contain. He rocked his own hips in time to match her strokes, his own pleasure mounting, until the only thing keeping him in check was the pain of the seam biting brutally into his crotch.

Michael didn't complain. He just rested his cheek on the top of her head and inhaled her familiar scent, fresh and feminine and somehow earthy like the outdoors. He let the pain control the ache, surging and receding. He touched and caressed his beautiful wife until she trembled against him, and the sounds of her shallow breathing echoed through the twilight.

Michael reacted instinctively. He knew this woman, sensed her responses almost before she responded. He touched her in places that made her shiver, made her move against him to knead her orgasm into breaking.

And when his own ache became too much, when he had to distract himself by touching her, he caught her arms and wheeled her around, crowded her back against the stall door.

Then he lowered his face and kissed his name from her lips, speared his tongue inside her mouth, explored her soft sighs and longing moans. He shared his own need by pressing up against her, dragging his hands over every wet delicious inch of her.

But Jillian's hands were free now, too. She dragged them down his back, sank her fingers into his ass and pulled him impossibly closer, until he groaned in frustration.

"Get naked," she whispered against his mouth.

No way in hell. And if she could talk, then he wasn't doing his job properly. Or had he heard her thoughts?

Michael couldn't tell, so he didn't reply. He only sank his hand between them, slithered his fingers between her thighs. He broke their kiss and dragged his mouth down her throat, along the pulse beating there.

Then he zeroed in on his target.

Sucking a tight peak into his mouth with a deliberate

stroke, he tasted wet fabric and warm skin, felt a moment of pure male satisfaction when Jillian shivered, rode his hand trying to capture him inside.

But the satisfaction was short-lived. The taste of her flooded his senses, spiked his need until he wasn't sure how long he would stay standing. Her rocking hips built the pressure of that seam to unholy agony, but it was a bittersweet pleasure-pain, arousing as much as it paralyzed.

He found her wet and ready. Pressing a finger inside, he felt her clench in a burst of moist heat. She let out a low moan and took her pleasure with a boldness that made him ache as she came apart in his arms.

She clung to him, lifeless, her breaths ragged. His own broken breathing mingled with hers in the quiet. Their hearts raced together as he willed himself to remain standing, willed her not to move and test his strength.

Horses whinnied and twilight lengthened the shadows, cooling the temperature with the approach of night, a connection to reality during a moment that felt too pleasurable, too powerful to be anything but the best fantasy.

And when he finally managed his own ache, could breathe again without the seam of his jeans threatening permanent damage, Michael noticed the trough overflowing from the hose he'd left in it. "Damn, your shoes aren't the only wet ones."

# *12*

BY THE TIME they made it up to the hayloft to reenact a long-ago make-out session, Jillian realized this weekend wasn't playing out according to her plan, sexy lingerie or not.

She'd intended to bring Michael to his knees, but for some reason, Michael seemed solely intent upon her pleasure. Every time she tried to take control, she wound up gasping and boneless from another incredible orgasm.

Not that she was complaining, of course.

Sometime between three—or was it four?—orgasms later, twilight deepened and the moon rose on a moonlit night alive with sounds of the forest. Wildlife scurried into the underbrush, settling in for sleep. A lone owl hooted. Frogs croaked and cicadas sang.

She and Michael might have been alone in a world where the only thing that mattered was pleasure. There was no work or obligation or routine. Their world was filled with familiar and inviting sounds, a world where the past and present collided.

Once upon a time, they'd sneaked into this very loft to make out. In broad daylight, too, which had been risky since Ike wandered in and out of this barn on whim. But when one of the campers had gone through a rotted plank on the dock during the morning water-skiing session, Ike had hustled to repair it before the afternoon session began.

As soon as they'd heard the news, she and Michael had slipped from the group of riders who'd been saddling up for a trail ride, and climbed up into the hayloft for some long-awaited and much anticipated privacy.

Jillian remembered the passion of that day, found the same passion tonight, only with it a pleasure that had matured through the years, a pleasure only possible when two people intimately knew one another, trusted one another, understood the power of placing their lover's desires above their own.

Michael was intent on pleasuring her tonight, on recreating their memory of the hayloft with the skill of a long-time lover. Jillian proved powerless to resist the magic she'd only ever known in his arms, and she surrendered to pleasure.

And when he'd annihilated her nearly past the point of no return, she attempted to divest her lusty husband of his pants, knowing that if she didn't turn the tables now, she risked slipping into an orgasm-induced coma, from which she had no clue when—or if—she'd awaken.

But Michael resisted. "Uh-uh."

"I can't take off your pants?"

"No." His gaze smoldered, intense and strangely unfamiliar in the starlit shadows.

"Why?"

"If you take off my pants, I won't be able to resist you."

"That's the point."

Sinking back into the hay, he stretched his arms over his head, treating her to the starlit version of a very attractive stomach and chest showing the effects of his recent lifestyle changes. "Your point maybe, but not mine."

"What's your point then?"

"To pleasure you."

"For how long?"

"However long it takes."

"However long *what* takes?"

He chuckled. "Trust me. Now why don't you just lie down here and let me hold you?"

"If I lie down, I'll pass out."

"That's a problem?"

She shoved the hair from her face, the simple act an effort of will with arms still languid and heavy from pleasure. "You've nearly put me in a coma."

"That's why you need to come here."

"But if I don't get those pants off you, I won't stand a chance of winning this game tonight." And Jillian needed to win. She had plans for this weekend, *important* plans, and they revolved around getting this man naked and orgasmic.

"Depends on what you consider winning. How many times have you climaxed?"

He had an answer for everything tonight.

"If your parts don't get air, they'll shrivel up and fall off."

He gave a whistle. "That's a low blow."

"A low blow? Sounds like a great idea—if you take your pants off."

"Not yet, sugar." Grabbing the saddle blanket, he pulled it over his legs. "So why don't you stop asking all these questions, snuggle up in my arms and let those eyes close. You're plum exhausted from all those orgasms."

Jillian wanted to know what was on his mind, needed to know to alter her plans if they needed altering, but she simply didn't have the energy to resist sinking into his warm embrace.

By the time she opened her eyes again, a rooster crowed the dawn and she had straw in her hair. And a few other choice places, too.

But Michael was there, on his knees and looking dream-like in the predawn haze, helping her sit up with one hand and offering her a mug of steaming coffee with the other.

"Where'd you go?" She sounded sleepy and wasted.

"Ran to Ike's. It was close." He raised the mug to her lips.

Leaning into his embrace, she sipped, letting the vestiges of sleep fall away beneath the surge of hot caffeine. The predawn bathed the loft in a gray haze, the sounds of life awakening outdoors lending the moment a surreal quality. She felt wistful and content, sitting there in his arms, her body coming to life with the achy remind-ers of last night's intimacy.

She felt hopeful. Not only because the weekend was off to a good start, but because she hoped they would turn a corner in their marriage and head down a path that would renew their involvement with each other. While they were exploring fantasies and sharing pleasure, they could bridge the distance that had been growing between them so things like her health issues and his lifestyle changes wouldn't seem to come out of the blue.

The timing was perfect. They were out of their routine and feeling relaxed. They were focused solely on each other in a way they hadn't been since their college days.

Now they just needed to make love.

She wanted Michael to feel as wonderful and content as she did right now. And her awakening brain cells recalled the limitations he'd imposed last night. They couldn't make love until she got his pants off....

"I'm awake now." Tipping her head back, she gazed at him and found him frowning. "What's wrong?"

He just shook his head and said, "Sugar, we've got a farm to tend."

With that, he was on his feet, herding Jillian into action so fast that she had to suck down the last few swallows of coffee before he snatched the mug away. They dug through the hay to find her clothes.

"Did I tell you how much I like your new outfit?" He handed her a twist of clingy fabric that turned out to be her bottoms.

She shook out the shorts before attempting to put them on. "Several times, in fact. You should see what else I have."

"Sexy like this?" He held up her top.

"I was inspired."

"Lucky me."

"You'll never know unless we get those pants off."

He only laughed and headed down the ladder.

Jillian followed.

"I was such an idiot the last time we were up in this loft," he said when she was about halfway down.

"Why's that?"

"Because I had no idea what the view was like from down here."

"If memory serves, I had jeans on the last time I made this climb."

"If I'd have had any idea what you'd look like with your long bare legs and that sweet bottom, I'd have taken those jeans off myself."

"If memory serves, you did."

He laughed. "But I'd have thrown them over the edge so you'd have had to climb down to get them."

Jillian didn't get a chance to reply. As soon as her feet hit the ground, Michael swept her into his arms, and she found herself colliding against warm, hard male.

Warm, hard *aroused* male.

"Sure you don't want to lose the jeans yet?"

"*Want* has nothing to do with it."

She dropped open-mouthed kisses from his throat to his shoulder, determined to distract him from his sudden diligence. And she thought she'd accomplished her goal. He shuddered and exhaled a contented sigh. Then he spun her around and marched straight out of the barn to the chicken coop.

They split the chore list down the middle. Soon Jillian was back inside the still-damp sandals. But even that sensation faded from her awareness as she fed the farm animals, starting with the chickens and ending with the goats, where one kid trailed behind her, more interested in nibbling the lace on her shorts than in breakfast.

She had to pay special attention to the newborn piglets, but they all seemed to be thriving. By the time she completed her share of the chores, the sun shone brightly overhead and her stomach growled hungrily.

"Ready for breakfast?" She caught up with Michael at the lake where he was feeding the ducks.

"I guess. These guys sure are. I can't believe Ike feeds them. You'd think there was enough food around here between the forest and the lake."

"He supplements their diet with vitamins and minerals

to keep them healthy," she explained. "But you're not hungry, Michael? We haven't eaten since lunch yesterday."

"Pshaw. I ate my fill of you last night, sugar," he said. "You're an outdoors gal. Why don't you just slip up under old Bessie and have a sip of fresh milk?"

"I was thinking more along the lines of a little protein and a lot of caffeine. I'm still not awake."

Michael ruffled his fingers through her hair, making even more of a mess. "But I like you looking all soft and sleepy. Makes me think about snuggling between your warm thighs."

"No more snuggling until I get a shower. I'm covered in corn dust from the chicken scratch."

"I like corn."

"Uh-uh, buddy. If you won't take your jeans off, then I've got nothing stopping me from taking a shower."

Jillian turned around to head back to the house, but suddenly Michael's arms came around her. She gasped and tried to break away, but he had her off her feet in an instant.

Ducks scattered in a flurry of outraged squawks and flapping wings as he strode toward the lake.

"Michael, no!"

Too late. They were airborne for a suspended instant before he twisted around to hit the water first. His body broke the impact, but he sank like a stone.

And Jillian sank with him.

The cold water closed over them like an icy blanket. The breath froze in her lungs, and she might have been naked for all the good her skimpy outfit did at keeping her warm. Her sandals proved the final insult as the water sucked them off. Each one surfaced in turn and floated idly out of reach.

Michael finally released her, and she broke the surface gasping and sputtering.

He came up right behind her, laughing, water sluicing over his bare chest, his jeans clinging to his butt sexily.

"Crazy man." She could barely get the words out. Every muscle in her body had seized in shock. "What are you doing?"

He stood in the thigh-high water, looking so much like the boy she'd once skinny-dipped with, his smile dashing, his blue eyes bright and his hair plastered to his head. She didn't think to resist when he pulled her into his arms.

"Come here, Jilly, I'll make you warm."

Their bodies came together in a collision of cold, wet skin. They melded together the way they always did, aligned as though they'd been designed for each other.

Despite the chill, everything inside Jillian melted on a wave of awareness, the silk of his wet skin and his strong arms cradling her close. Suddenly his mouth came down on hers and he dragged his tongue across her lower lip.

"I love you," he said huskily. "Have I told you yet today?"

Closing her eyes, she clung to him as she had so long ago, as if she never wanted to let him go, as if the precious moments they shared together were all too fleeting. This urgency might have faded through the years, a feeling that each moment was unique and meant to be savored, never wasted.

But she remembered now. The problems they had were so minor in the scheme of their lives, the scales tipped toward good fortune and blessings. Jillian could hardly believe she'd let such stupid things like missed birthdays and forgotten doctors' appointments gain so much momentum in her head.

No more. She had too much to be grateful for. This wonderful man loved her. He'd dieted and exercised because he wanted to look good for her. He'd plotted fantasies because he missed her. No, he wasn't perfect, but then neither was she.

They were only perfect for each other.

She'd let that be enough.

Jillian had missed him, and hadn't realized just how much until he'd shown up in their driveway on a chopper. Until he'd cornered her inside his office with nipple clamps. Until he'd pleasured her in a hayloft. Until he kissed her now with a wild abandon that assured her he'd missed her as much.

They'd tackled tough problems before. They'd tackle this, too. If she could just get those pants off...

Molding her hands over his shoulders and down his arms, she glided each deliberate stroke over his wet skin, raising goose bumps in her wake. Parting her thighs around his, Jillian rode against him, earning a heated response when he dragged his hands down her back and sank his fingers into her bottom.

He ground against her, the bulge trapped inside wet jeans swelling hungrily, his need breaking in a low growl against her mouth. Jillian kissed the sound from his lips, let her hands roam freely over his bare chest, grazing hard nipples through the crisp smattering of chest hairs over them.

She trailed kisses from his lips, along his stubbled jaw. She savored the taste of him, sampled the eagerness of his arousal, shared her own awakening need.

With a laugh, Michael speared his hands into her hair and

arched her head until he could give back in kind. Dragging open-mouthed kisses down her throat, he joined in on the frenzy of the moment, his hands roaming, his hips arching, his laughter breaking as warm bursts against her skin.

Then he broke away, diving cleanly into the water.

"Michael!" She dove in after him, finding the depths a warmer refuge than the air.

They played chase in a game from long ago. She swam after Michael, who paused only long enough for her to almost catch up before taking off again.

They'd played this game at every birthday and pool party they'd ever attended together while growing up.

Once they'd grown up, they'd played the game again as eager young lovers.

Now they were back again. Her muscles strained and warmed with the freedom of the activity, waking her more surely than any amount of caffeine. She cast off even the achy tenderness of the night before as laughter and adrenaline rushed through her, the challenge of catching her playful husband and finally, *finally* coaxing his jeans off.

And when at last he made it back to the dock, he hoisted himself up before assisting her. She stretched out beside him, grateful for the rising sun that warmed them, breathless and excited and more relaxed than she could remember being in far too long.

"Will you let me get those jeans off you?" she asked after catching her breath.

"Persistent, aren't you?"

"That shouldn't come as a surprise. We can't make love until you take your pants off."

"Horny, aren't you?"

"Mmm-hmm," she agreed boldly.

He only laughed, and she reached out to brush away trickles of water running from his hair along his cheek.

"No, I'm not surprised you're so persistent, Jilly. You've been tagging after me trying to get me to pay attention to you since I was in kindergarten."

"Sorry?"

"Only that it took me until high school to notice you as more than Donny's pesky kid sister. I wasted way too much time."

She liked his answer. "We'll just have to make up for that time now."

"Sounds like a good plan." He rolled to his side and propped up on an elbow, gazing down at her with such utter seriousness that her breath caught. "I can be such an idiot when it comes to you."

"What are you talking about?"

"Your mammogram."

Oh. "You want to talk about it?"

He nodded.

Jillian had made her choices and would stand by them, even though she recognized the hurt in his face and how hard he tried to hide it. "How'd you find out?"

"Your films are in the office. Are you surprised I noticed them?"

There was no place to go with that question except for the truth. She just nodded her assent.

"I'm *not* surprised by that."

"I wasn't trying to hide anything, Michael. I just wasn't ready to discuss what was going on."

"Why?"

The moment of truth. Jillian hesitated, not wanting to spoil the contentment of this sunny morning, the memories of a past that made her feel so close to him. She didn't want anger to put more distance between them. She was so tired of distance. She'd wanted to seduce him senseless before they tackled this, but the choice was no longer hers.

Michael must have recognized her uncertainty because he reached for her hand, a loving gesture of reassurance. "Give it to me straight. I can handle it. I *want* to handle it."

There was something so earnest in his voice…. Staring down at their clasped hands, she drew strength from the sight of his strong fingers threaded through hers.

How did she tell him that she felt as if her health didn't matter to him? She'd had this conversation so many times in her head, but now that she needed to open her mouth, everything she wanted to say sounded resentful and petty, would surely put him on the defense.

"You were hurt because I never asked how your appointments went, weren't you."

There was no question in his voice, or any accusation, either. Just a simple statement of fact. And to Jillian's shame, she felt utterly relieved that he understood and she didn't have to explain it. She knew how much Michael hated disappointing her. And she hated making him feel that way. She hated feeling guilty for wanting something from him.

"I was wrong, Jilly," he said quietly. "Don't feel bad about that."

"I wasn't playing games," she said. "I just needed to sort

through my feelings. I certainly didn't expect an abnormal result, and needed to deal with that. But I was hurt. I felt like you should have cared enough to express some interest. I hated feeling so resentful. That's why I chose not to say anything yet. I needed to wait until I got my feelings under control, or else I knew I'd make you feel guilty."

He dropped his gaze to their clasped hands, and she knew he was looking for that same refuge and strength in their clasped hands. She gave a reassuring squeeze.

"I should feel guilty for not asking how your appointments went. It's not that I don't care about your health. I hope you'll believe that. It's just I always assume you'll tell me anything that's important. I count on it too much. I didn't realize it until now, and that's just not fair."

"Of course I know you care, Michael. I also know you're busy. Our lives get so hectic sometimes—"

"Nothing is more important to me than you are. If I've let other things get in the way of me showing you, then I'm wrong. I appreciate you always rising to my defense, but I don't want you making excuses for my behavior. It's not fair to either of us."

She thought about that. And he was right. She did make excuses for his behavior. She defended him against her own allegations of thoughtlessness then felt guilty because she wanted simple consideration.

"I should have told you how I felt and not expected you to be a mind reader."

Something about that made him smile. "Yes, you should have."

He didn't give her a chance to respond but rolled toward her. Pulling her into his arms, he tucked her close until they were cheek to cheek. "I've gotten complacent. I don't know exactly when it happened, but it did. About our marriage. About my health. About *your* health. You have every right to be upset with me. I haven't been there for you, and I'm sorry. I want to change this. But I'll need your help. And I'm talking about more than your slick moves in the kitchen. Don't think I haven't noticed you don't buy snacks anymore."

She chuckled. "I just want you to be healthy. I worry about how you're tired all the time."

"Then *tell* me. I want you to share what's going on inside your pretty head. Now I'm paying attention, I get the feeling that what you say and what you think don't always add up."

If he only knew… "Are you angry I didn't tell you about my test results?"

"Yes, but not at you. I understand how you felt. I placed you in a position where you have every right to feel hurt. But because you love me, you kept worrying more about my reactions than how wrong I was being to you." He pressed a kiss to the top of her head. "I'm glad you love me."

Tipping her head back, she gazed into his face, needed to see the regret in his bright eyes, needed to feel the hope of his words. "You know, sometimes I think you are a mind reader. That's exactly how I feel."

He laughed. Then, rolling onto his back, he pulled her on top of him so she lay draped over him like a curvy blanket, their bodies aligning in exactly the right places. "If I apologize and ask nicely, will you tell me what's going on?"

"I've got a lump. It looks like a fibroadenoma, and three doctors have told me not to worry. The edges are clearly defined, so they're pretty sure it's benign. They won't know for certain until they biopsy it. I'm comfortable with that."

"Not worried?"

"How about not worried *a lot?*"

He pressed a kiss to her brow. "Have you scheduled the procedure?"

"No. Not until I talked to you. I intended to make love to you this weekend and when you were brain-dead and boneless, I was going to tell you."

"Guess I messed up your plan."

"I'm not complaining." She smiled. "I haven't scheduled the surgery yet because I want you to be with me. I wasn't sure if you'd want to close the office or ask Dr. Cavanaugh to cover with your patients."

"I'd rather close the office. I'm sure Charlotte and the girls won't mind a day off."

"Not as long as you pay them."

"Naturally." He dragged his hands down her back, a tender caress that awakened such heat inside her. "I want you to expect from me, Jillian, and I want you to tell me what you expect. I need you to."

He watched her with a gaze that left no room for doubts, saw the truth of a love that was still growing, still as promising as it had always been.

She sighed. "I love you, Michael."

He caught her mouth in a kiss that promised her forever, and she looped her arms around his neck, taking advantage of her superior position, loving the sun warming her back, the sounds of the wildlife and the lapping water, the feel of Michael's hands on her.

She knew that they could handle whatever came up, if

they handled it together. No more holding out, no more resentment, no more hurt feelings. Everything suddenly felt right in her world. Except for one thing…

Wrapping her arms around Michael's waist, she anchored herself close and gave a heave with all her might.

"Jilly!" His muscles gathered as he vainly resisted the move that toppled them right off the dock.

*Splash.*

Jillian slithered away before Michael came up sputtering.

"What are you—"

She caught him by the waistband of his jeans and helped him stand. "There's a fantasy I have that I haven't told you about yet. Since you're not a mind reader, I thought I'd show you, but it involves taking off these pants."

His bright eyes sparkled. Bracing his elbows on the dock, he hoisted himself up enough so she could work the sodden tangle of his jeans and briefs down his legs.

It took a little while and a good bit of effort, but by the time she dragged the last of his clothes away, she'd unleashed what had grown into a raging erection.

"Looks like you have the same fantasy." She was about to break away, but he caught her arms and pulled her close.

"Oh, I do." He made quick work of her lingerie, and then both of them stood face to face with the water lapping between them, finally naked.

Jillian rested her head against his chest, caught up in the moment. Gliding her tongue in the scoop between his neck and shoulder, she sampled the fresh-water taste of him.

"I want you to remember all the reasons why you fell in love with me." He pressed tender kisses into her hair and along her temple.

"I've never forgotten. You know that, don't you?"

When he gazed down into her face with all the love she felt mirrored in his eyes, Jillian knew she'd said the right thing.

"I do."

"Good." She broke out of his embrace and bolted away in a wild attempt to gain distance. "If you can catch me, you can have me." She called out the dare over her shoulder.

With his husky laughter echoing over the lake, Michael dove in after her.

And one of those reasons was that he was a much faster swimmer.

# *13*

*Three weeks later*

SERAFINE HAD TO do a little fancy talking to convince the floor nurse she was a family member checking in on Mrs. Jillian. But the nurse had been smart enough to know Serafine wasn't going to budge from that desk until she saw the patient.

"The doctor just examined her, so she'll be released soon," the nurse explained as she directed Serafine through the corridor of recovery rooms.

"Guess I won't be long visiting then."

The nurse frowned disapprovingly. She gave a sharp knock before opening the door and announcing, "You have a visitor."

Holding the door wide, she allowed Serafine to enter. Tucking her picnic basket close, she smiled when she saw Mrs. Jillian on the bed already dressed, and Dr. Michael seated beside her, his arm wrapped around her shoulders.

"Well, don't you two lovebirds look right as rain?"

"Widow Serafine," Mrs. Jillian sounded as sleepy as her heavy-lidded eyes looked, but her smile was genuine, which made Serafine glad she'd bullied the old nurse. "What are you doing here? Is everything okay at the camp?"

"Never better. All one hundred and three of our little campers are wreaking havoc on the hallowed grounds as we speak. I snuck away to check up on you. We were all worried."

"You didn't need to drive all the way down." Dr. Michael's welcoming smile convinced her he wasn't sorry she had.

"Of course I did." She held up a huge picnic basket. "Marie-Louise and I cooked up enough food so you won't have to cook for a week. It's all on ice in here, so never you mind about it. Just toss the basket in the car, Dr. Michael. It'll stay all day. Unload everything into the fridge after you get Mrs. Jillian home and settled."

"Thank you," they both said.

Serafine set the basket on the floor beside the door. "Got all your favorites, too. Gumbo, fried chicken, bouillabaisse, and Marie-Louise whipped up two pies—raisin and pecan."

Dr. Michael groaned. "My diet's going straight to hell this week. That's for sure."

"Diet?" Serafine eyed him like a Christmas goose. "Why would you be dieting? Strapping boy like you needs meat on your bones. Gotta keep up your strength. That right, Mrs. Jillian?"

Jillian just smiled.

"Well, I won't be keeping you two. Just wanted to drop off the basket and see you with my own eyes."

"Would you let everyone know the surgery went well?" Dr. Michael asked. "Ike asked me to call specifically."

"Of course, I'll take care of it. Don't give it another thought. We're all worried about Mrs. Jillian."

Jillian shook her head. "No more worrying. The surgeon got everything and said it all looks benign. Of course, we'll know for sure in ten days after the radiologist does the biopsy, but so far so good."

"Praise the Lord." Serafine meant it. This young couple had love on their side. They should be together for long lifetimes, raising babies and staring at each other all starry-eyed.

Dr. Michael pressed a kiss on his wife's tousled head. "That goes for you, Jilly. No more worrying."

"That's right, Mrs. Jillian." Serafine backed him up. "You need to be recovering your strength from the surgery. Don't tell me you're worried about the camp. We've got it well in hand."

"Oh, I know that," Jillian said quickly.

"No question there, Widow Serafine," Dr. Michael explained. "That's what has Jillian worried. You're doing such a wonderful job with the campers that she's worrying what'll happen when your family rebuilds your home. We've been tossing around ideas to make you want to stay at the camp."

Serafine couldn't help but laugh. Somehow things always worked out in the end, didn't they? "Well, funny you'd mention that. My kin and I have been tossing around some ideas, too. Raphael's been worried you won't need all of them once they get the place shipshape again. As they've settled in better than I could have ever hoped, we've been talking about ways to make ourselves useful after the campers leave."

"The positions are year-round." Mrs. Jillian sounded all brisk and businesslike, but she looked sleepy and worried. "The farm is busy all through the school year. I know Ike needs the help, and I don't see any reason why you all can't train to conduct tours and parties if you're of a mind to learn. Raphael, Philip and Marie-Louise would be naturals."

"Now don't you be thinking about anything except getting better right now, Mrs. Jillian," Serafine ordered gently. "We Baptistes signed on for the long haul, don't you know it. Raphael's just looking to make himself and his kin so useful you won't feel like they're slacking. He likes it there right well. They all do."

"What sort of ideas did you all come up with?" Dr. Michael asked. "Why don't you sit and tell us?"

Serafine shook her head. "We can get together and talk about things when Mrs. Jillian's up to par again. But to give you an idea, we've been looking into college. Working at Camp Cavelier might make my kin eligible for some historic-preservation and wildlife-conservation scholarships. Raphael's thinking about business management so he can run the place proper. Marie-Louise is a shoo-in for hospitality management and, believe it or not, Philip has quite a head for numbers. He's already burning a sign for an office door. It says, Philip Baptiste, Chief Financial Officer."

Both Mrs. Jillian and Dr. Michael laughed.

"Sounds like we'd have all the bases covered," Dr. Michael said with a twinkle in those big baby blues.

"Seems that way to me," Serafine agreed. "But there'll be plenty of time to talk once Mrs. Jillian's on the mend and the campers go home. So put your minds at rest."

Mrs. Jillian smiled softly. "But what about you, Widow Serafine? Don't you miss your family?"

"Well, sure I do." She folded her arms across her chest and darted a meaningful gaze between husband and wife. "I like having everyone within easy reach, but it's not like Bayou Doré is that far away. Do my kin a world of good to get out and see me for a change, I'm thinking. Teach 'em to appreciate me." She grinned. "Virginie's brood is my kin, too, and doesn't look like getting around has done them any harm."

What she'd keep to herself for the moment was that Raphael was right about something else. She *was* sweet on Ike, in a way she'd never been sweet on her late husband.

God bless his soul.

"Camp Cavelier needs the Baptistes. Just look at Ike in that lonely cabin of his with instant coffee and microwave dinners." Serafine shook her head. "That's no way for a man to live. Especially not a man who works as hard as he does."

Mrs. Jillian and Dr. Michael exchanged surprised looks, *knowing* looks.

Serafine just smiled. Well, could she help it if she was beginning to see why her baby sister had been so fond of adventuring? Who knew she'd turn out to be a late bloomer?

Virginie was probably laughing her fool head off.

"Ike's been a good influence on the boys," Serafine said with a wink.

"I'm sure he is," Dr. Michael said.

"Well, now that that's all settled, I guess I'll be heading back. You take good care of each other, and don't worry about the camp. We've got it under control."

"Thanks so much for everything," Mrs. Jillian said.

"You both, too. You've been good to me and my kin, and we appreciate it. Just holler if you need anything else."

Serafine paused in the doorway and turned back to them. "Oh, Dr. Michael. I was meaning to tell you that this bridge of mine is doing the job just great."

"Glad to hear it."

"And I wanted to ask…what's going on with that new crown of yours? Is it defective or something?

Dr. Michael's eyes widened, and he opened his mouth when Jillian caught his chin in her hand and tipped his face toward her for a look.

"What's the matter with it?" she asked.

"The color is way off from his other pretty teeth. I noticed it from this doorway, and my eyesight isn't the best."

Serafine didn't need the best eyesight to see understanding dawning on Dr. Michael's face.

He met her gaze and smiled. "It must be defective then. I'll take care of it as soon as I get back to the office. Thanks for mentioning it."

Serafine inclined her head in approval and turned to leave. She was going home. Everything was going to turn out just right for the Landrys, and Virginie's brood, and for her, too.

She *knew* it.

*When the trouble was over and done with*

MICHAEL INSPECTED the small porcelain tooth, wondering whether or not he should save it for another day. Who knew what life might serve up and when a superpower might come in handy? And his superpower had proven much better than any super-improved brain power. Who wanted to outthink everyone on the planet when he'd been able to read the mind of the only woman who'd ever mattered in his life?

And when that woman showed up in the doorway of the exam room, silhouetted by the shadows of the dark hallway behind her, his gut gave a hard twist at the sight.

Jillian looked so beautiful with reddish-blond hair waving around her face, her gaze caressing him in warm recognition, an expression that mirrored everything he felt inside. She flashed him a high-beam smile that twisted his gut a little more....

It had been this way between them ever since their return from their fantasy weekend at Camp Cavelier. They'd come up with a working solution to growing apart, and were committed to carrying it out. He'd been amazed at how much time they'd found to enjoy being together in the weeks since. When the emphasis was where it belonged—on each other—everything else seemed to be fading back where it belonged.

He was also amazed at how much he enjoyed finding new things to notice about this beautiful and competent woman he loved, and how much he enjoyed making her happy. There were definite perks to a happy Jillian, because the more he tried to please her, the more she tried to please him.

"What are you doing?" she asked.

"Testing out the bite on my new crown."

"You ordered a new one?"

He nodded.

"I really don't know what Widow Serafine was talking about. I didn't see a thing wrong with the color."

He shrugged. "It can't hurt. I'm tired of thinking about my teeth. Spend enough time thinking about my patients."

"And you need plenty of time to think about me." She swept inside the exam room and crowded against him.

Michael set the crown on the counter and wrapped his arms around her. "I do think about you. All the time."

He was paying attention to things he'd never noticed

about her before, more than just reading her mind. They'd been married for seven years, yet, until recently, he'd never noticed the way she followed him with her eyes whenever he walked into a room. The way she blushed whenever he caught her watching. Jillian seemed to be ever-growing and ever-changing, and Michael knew he could make a lifetime study of her if he kept his eyes open.

He wanted that lifetime.

She'd recovered quickly from surgery, and the biopsy results confirmed what the doctors had suspected—the tumor had been benign. She'd have to undergo annual exams to ensure that another didn't crop up and go undetected, but that was a result they would gratefully live with.

Michael had also taken it upon himself to research holistic approaches to staying healthy and had been working behind the scenes to ensure they implemented them.

One of the biggest suppressants of the immune system was stress, so he'd been keeping a close eye on Jillian's schedule and using a variety of distractions to keep her from piling too much on her plate. Sex topped the list. As always, she was a very accommodating wife, and if she could cross junk food off her grocery list without mentioning it…

"You think about me when you're working?" Jillian asked.

"I listen for your voice when you're talking to patients. I can even tell when you're coming down the hall."

She arched an eyebrow. "The floor's laminate and every one of us wears rubber-soled shoes."

"Didn't I ever mention that your legs are one of my favorite parts of your body? I know I must have. I've been noticing the way you walk since high school. You have a certain pace, all quick and light. I know it's you. I'm never wrong."

"Never?"

He brushed a silky wave from her temple. "Never. I look up, and there you are in the doorway, smiling that smile that makes me weak in the knees."

"Weak in the knees? Right. Horny is more like it."

"That's a given."

"Speaking of... I've been thinking lately, Michael. Since you've been making all my fantasies come true, I should reciprocate, don't you think? Only seems fair."

He'd spent so much time thinking about Jillian's fantasies that if he'd had to name a fantasy of his own, he couldn't have. "What do you know about my fantasies?"

"Not enough, unfortunately, but that's something I think we should address." She stepped out of his arms, and her eyes glinted with a familiar playfulness that he was seeing more and more frequently lately.

She backed away, reaching for the button at her throat with a deliberate motion. "That seems to be the place to start. Besides, I'm not totally in the dark. I do know a few things."

"You read minds?"

She shook her head, sending glossy waves tumbling around her shoulders in a move that made him imagine running his fingers through her hair, over her smooth skin and all those sleek curves... "Then what do you know?"

"Your fantasies involve me."

"That they do."

She turned her attention to sliding out of her uniform top, which suddenly didn't look nearly so professional with a lacy bra and expanse of smooth stomach taunting him from between the parted fabric.

"Have I mentioned how much I like all your new lingerie? I need to remember to send Stephanie something at Christmas to thank her."

"She'll like that. She's been contributing to my delinquency since the ninth grade."

Michael laughed and would have made a crack about Stephanie's own delinquency taming into domesticity through the years, except that his mouth suddenly went dry when Jillian let her smock slither to the floor.

Her bra followed.

She stood there tantalizingly bare from the waist up, breasts swaying on her every breath. Michael folded his arms across his chest and leaned against the counter to enjoy the show, enjoying the way her breasts plumped forward invitingly when she leaned forward to shimmy her pants down.

"You're sure the office is locked up, Jilly? I'd hate for one of the staff to realize she'd forgotten something and come back. We won't hear her until it is way too late."

"Charlotte never forgets anything. And neither Dianne nor Brandi would come back even if they did. They want out of here at the end of the day."

"Bold words."

She only smiled. "That's something else I think you like."

"What?"

"When I'm bold."

"Right again." His body temperature went on a steady rise as she did a sexy shimmy to ease her pants over her hips, revealing a tiny scrap of lacy pink fabric between her thighs.

He was *definitely* sending Stephanie a gift.

But that was his last thought as his brain short-circuited.

Jillian kicked her pants off to reveal those long, long legs that had admittedly been a part of his fantasies since as far back as he could remember.

"I'll bet you're thinking about my legs wrapped around your waist right now, aren't you, Michael?"

"So you *are* a mind reader." He was impressed with himself for getting the words out.

She just laughed, a silky purr that crossed the distance between them as if it were alive... Then she leaned over to grab her pants off the floor, treating him to the sight of her firm bottom in nothing but that teensy thong. Bracing his hands on the counter, he stared at the sight of the two dimples above her cheeks and the thin strap that disappeared in between.

His body went on red alert and his memory flooded with the knowledge of what her skin would feel like to his touch. Thanks to diet and exercise, he felt better than he had in a long time. He and Jillian had certainly been enjoying more sex than they had in forever, so why was he standing there with a hard-on like it was the first time he'd ever seen her naked?

He wanted to push off the counter, but his arms wouldn't cooperate. His heart pounded. His pulse throbbed so hard in his ears he almost missed it when she said in a voice that was pure temptation, "Your turn."

She sauntered toward him, all sleek curves and bold purpose. Then she started unbuttoning his lab coat.

Ah, his turn to get naked.

Michael managed to rally himself enough to lend his effort to the cause. Their hands brushed together, fingers entwined as they divested him of his lab coat, his shirt, then went to work on his pants.

Jillian pressed small kisses over his chest as she freed his erection. "Mmm. Someone's happy to see me."

"Damn straight."

She slid her silken fingers along his hot skin, which jerked greedily in reply.

"Come here, Michael." She led him toward his dental chair with her hand still firmly on his dick.

He could tell by the tone of her voice that she had something very specific in mind, but Michael couldn't seem to rally up the energy to ask what it might be. He was more than content to let Jillian have her way with him, and found himself being pushed into his chair, much as she'd been in a fantasy he'd attempted to create not so long ago—before he'd honed his skills at creating fantasies.

"You think my fantasy is to make love in my dental chair?" he asked to distract himself from the heat that was singeing his crotch. "We already did this."

"You're right. Sort of." She pressed him back. He obliged, stretching out, wincing as his naked ass squeaked on the pleather. "I think your fantasy is for me to get bold while *you're* in the chair."

He didn't get a chance to imagine those possibilities before she got the jump on him. The next thing Michael knew he was handcuffed to the chair.

"We have definitely done this before."

"Sort of." She eyed him boldly while reclining the chair, but every inch he went back tested his shoulder socket.

"Hey, this is a strange position. Did your arm hurt when I had you cuffed like this?"

She just smiled. "Trust me, in a few minutes you won't remember you even have an arm."

Her words sent a sizzle of anticipation through him, and while he couldn't hear Jillian's thoughts right now, he was content to read all her sexy intentions in her warm eyes.

Michael didn't know if Widow Serafine's magic would last forever, but when he thought about the promises he and Jillian had made to each other about being open and putting their relationship ahead of everything else in their lives, he knew those promises would last a lifetime.

And that was when he decided to trash the crown. Just as soon as they finished playing out what was shaping up to be one hell of a fantasy...

\* \* \* \* \*

*Experience the anticipation, the thrill of the chase and
the sheer rush of falling in love!*
*Turn the page for a sneak preview of a new book from*
*Harlequin Romance*
***THE REBEL PRINCE***
*by Raye Morgan*
*On sale August 29th*
*wherever books are sold*

---

"Oh, no!"

The reaction slipped out before Emma Valentine could stop it, for there stood the very man she most wanted to avoid seeing again.

He didn't look any happier to see her.

"Well, come on, get on board," he said gruffly. "I won't bite." One eyebrow rose. "Though I might nibble a little," he added, mostly to amuse himself.

But she wasn't paying any attention to what he was saying. She was staring at him, taking in the royal blue uniform he was wearing, with gold braid and glistening badges decorating the sleeves, epaulettes and an upright collar. Ribbons and medals covered the breast of the short, fitted jacket. A gold-encrusted sabre hung at his side. And suddenly it was clear to her who this man really was.

She gulped wordlessly. Reaching out, he took her elbow and pulled her aboard. The doors slid closed. And finally she found her tongue.

"You…you're the prince."

He nodded, barely glancing at her. "Yes. Of course."

She raised a hand and covered her mouth for a moment. "I should have known."

"Of course you should have. I don't know why you didn't." He punched the ground-floor button to get the elevator moving again, then turned to look down at her. "A relatively bright five-year-old child would have tumbled to the truth right away."

Her shock faded as her indignation at his tone asserted itself. He might be the prince, but he was still just as annoying as he had been earlier that day.

"A relatively bright five-year-old child without a bump on the head from a badly thrown water polo ball, maybe," she said defensively. She wasn't feeling woozy any longer and she wasn't about to let him bully her, no matter how royal he was. "I was unconscious half the time."

"And just clueless the other half, I guess," he said, looking bemused.

The arrogance of the man was really galling.

"I suppose you think your 'royalness' is so obvious it sort of shimmers around you for all to see?" she challenged. "Or better yet, oozes from your pores like…like sweat on a hot day?"

"Something like that," he acknowledged calmly. "Most people tumble to it pretty quickly. In fact, it's hard to hide even when I want to avoid dealing with it."

"Poor baby," she said, still resenting his manner. "I guess that works better with injured people who are half asleep." Looking at him, she felt a strange emotion she couldn't identify. It was as though she wanted to prove something to him, but she wasn't sure what. "And anyway, you know you did your best to fool me," she added.

His brows knit together as though he really didn't know what she was talking about. "I didn't do a thing."

"You told me your name was Monty."

"It is." He shrugged. "I have a lot of names. Some of them are too rude to be spoken to my face, I'm sure." He glanced at her sideways, his hand on the hilt of his sabre. "Perhaps you're contemplating one of those right now."

*You bet I am.*

That was what she would like to say. But it suddenly occurred to her that she was supposed to be working for this man. If she wanted to keep the job of coronation chef, maybe she'd better keep her opinions to herself. So she clamped her mouth shut, took a deep breath and looked away, trying hard to calm down.

The elevator ground to a halt and the doors slid open laboriously. She moved to step forward, hoping to make her escape, but his hand shot out again and caught her elbow.

"Wait a minute. *You're* a woman," he said, as though that thought had just presented itself to him.

"That's a rare ability for insight you have there, Your Highness," she snapped before she could stop herself. And then she winced. She was going to have to do better than that if she was going to keep this relationship on an even keel.

But he was ignoring her dig. Nodding, he stared at her with a speculative gleam in his golden eyes. "I've been looking for a woman, but you'll do."

She blanched, stiffening. "I'll do for what?"

He made a head gesture in a direction she knew was opposite of where she was going and his grip tightened on her elbow.

"Come with me," he said abruptly, making it an order.

She dug in her heels, thinking fast. She didn't much like orders. "Wait! I can't. I have to get to the kitchen."

"Not yet. I need you."

"You what?" Her breathless gasp of surprise was soft, but she knew he'd heard it.

"I need you," he said firmly. "Oh, don't look so shocked. I'm not planning to throw you into the hay and have my way with you. I need you for something a bit more mundane than that."

She felt color rushing into her cheeks and she silently begged it to stop. Here she was, formless and stodgy in her chef's whites. No makeup, no stiletto heels. Hardly the picture of the femmes fatales he was undoubtedly used to. The likelihood that he would have any carnal interest in her was remote at best. To have him think she was hysterically defending her virtue was humiliating.

"Well, what if I don't want to go with you?" she said in hopes of deflecting his attention from her blush.

"Too bad."

"What?"

Amusement sparkled in his eyes. He was certainly enjoying this. And that only made her more determined to resist him.

"I'm the prince, remember? And we're in the castle. My orders take precedence. It's that old pesky divine rights thing."

Her jaw jutted out. Despite her embarrassment, she couldn't let that pass.

"Over my free will? Never!"

Exasperation filled his face.

"Hey, call out the historians. Someone will write a book about you and your courageous principles." His eyes glittered sardonically. "But in the meantime, Emma Valentine, you're coming with me."

# Forbidden Fantasy #4

## Knowing your lover's secret desires/fantasies

If you want to take your sex life to an exciting new realm, consider these tips for sparking the imagination:

**The Write Stuff**

Create a "fantasy grab bag" with your partner by each writing down various scenarios you would love to act out in the bedroom. Don't reveal your personal wish lists in advance. That way, when you select a slip of paper from the grab bag, one of you will always be surprised!

~or~

**Movie Night**

Rent a DVD that represents a genre you might have fun reenacting, be it a romantic costume drama or an edgy cop thriller. Once you and your sweetheart have finished your viewing party, the two of you can have fun thinking up your own sexy sequel!

*Sue Johanson is a registered nurse, sex educator, author and host of The Oxygen Network's* Talk Sex with Sue Johanson.

Photo courtesy of Oxygen Media, Inc.

**Silhouette**

**Desire**

**Introducing an exciting appearance
by legendary
*New York Times* bestselling author**

# DIANA PALMER

## HEARTBREAKER

He's the ultimate bachelor...
but he may have just met
the one woman to change his ways!

Join the drama in the story of a confirmed
bachelor, an amnesiac beauty and their
unexpected passionate romance.

---

**"Diana Palmer is a mesmerizing storyteller
who captures the essence of what
a romance should be."—*Affaire de Coeur***

---

**Heartbreaker *is available from Silhouette Desire
in September 2006.***

---

**Visit Silhouette Books at www.eHarlequin.com**   SDDPIBC

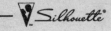
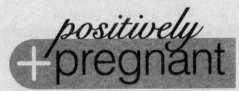

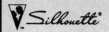

## HARLEQUIN®

# *Blaze*™

## COMING NEXT MONTH

### #273 MY ONLY VICE Elizabeth Bevarly

Rosie Bliss has a little thing for the police chief. Okay, it's more than a *little* thing. But when she propositions the guy, she gets a mixed message. His hands say yes, while his mouth says no. Lucky for her, she's a little hard of hearing....

### #274 FEAR OF FALLING Cindi Myers
*It Was a Dark And Sexy Night... Bk. 1*

As erotic artist John Sartain's business manager, Natalie Brighton has no intention of falling for him...even though something about him fascinates her. But when mysterious things start happening to her, she has to wonder if that fascination is worth her life...

### #275 INDULGE Nancy Warren
*For a Good Time, Call... Bk. 2*

What happens when you eat dessert...*before* dinner? Mercedes and J. D.'s relationship is only about sex—hot and plenty of it. Suddenly the conservative lawyer wants to change the rules and start over with a *date!* What gives?

### #276 JUST TRUST ME... Jacquie D'Alessandro
*Adrenaline Rush, Bk. 2*

Kayla Watson used to like traveling on business. But that was before her boss insisted she spy on scientist Brett Thorne on his trek into the Andes mountains. Now she's tired, dirty...and seriously in lust with sexy Brett. Lucky for her, he's lusting after her, too. But will it last when he finds out why she's there?

### #277 THE SPECIALIST Rhonda Nelson
*Men Out of Uniform, Bk. 2*

All's fair in love and war. That's Emma Langsford's motto. So when she's given the assignment of recovering a priceless military antique, nothing's going to stop her. And if sexy Brian Payne, aka The Specialist, gets in her way, she has ways of distracting him,....

### #278 ANYTHING FOR YOU Sarah Mayberry
*It's All About Attitude*

Delaney Michaels has loved Sam Kirk forever...but the man is too dense to notice! She wants more from life than this, so she's breaking free of Sam to start over. But just as she's making a clean getaway, he counters with a seductive suggestion she can't refuse!

**www.eHarlequin.com**